DOSH

Robert Swindells

DOSH

Hamish Hamilton · London

HAMISH HAMILTON LTD

Published by the Penguin Group
Penguin Books Ltd, 27 Wrights Lane, London w8 5tz, England
Penguin Putnam Inc., 375 Hudson Street, New York, New York 10014, USA
Penguin Books Australia Ltd, Ringwood, Victoria, Australia
Penguin Books Canada Ltd, 10 Alcorn Avenue, Toronto, Ontario, Canada m4v 3b2
Penguin Books (NZ) Ltd, Private Bag 102902, NSMC, Auckland, New Zealand

on the World Wide Web at: www.penguin.com

Penguin Books Ltd, Registered Offices: Harmondsworth, Middlesex, England

First published 1999
1 3 5 7 9 10 8 6 4 2

Copyright © Robert Swindells, 1999
All rights reserved

Set in 13/17pt Monotype Bembo
Typeset by Rowland Phototypesetting Ltd,
Bury St Edmunds, Suffolk
Printed in England by Clays Ltd, St Ives plc

British Library Cataloguing in Publication Data
A CIP catalogue record for this book is available from the British Library

ISBN 0-241-13936-8

ONE

Fax and Walkman corner Maisie Malin at break. These are not the boys' school names and this is not school business.

'Is it right what we heard?' goes Walkman. His hand on the wall keeps her corralled. She peers past his shoulder seeking help she knows won't come.

'Dunno. Depends what you heard, duntit?'

The other boy snickers. 'We heard you're starting with the pickles, kiddo. Tonight.'

Maisie nods. 'It's right then.'

'Who got you on?'

'My auntie. She's a line supervisor.'

'She could be the queen of frigging Sheba,' murmurs Walkman, 'you work, you tell us. You know that.'

'Yes, and I know why as well. Why should I give *you* ten per cent of my wages for nothing?'

Fax snorts. 'Why? Because that's the way things work. Always have, always will. And it's *not* for nothing. You get Push protection.'

'Oh I know, Push protects me from Push. *I*'ve seen all those gangster movies too. Well − I'm not paying and that's it.'

'Wouldn't be you then.'

'Give it a rest,' she sneers. 'You don't impress me with your daft nickname, Gordon Barraclough. Fax! *Fix*'d be nearer the mark for a crackhead like you. And as for *you* –' she turns to Longstaff – 'I see you as Dorkman rather than Walkman, and the Push sound like a sixties rock band.'

'Oh, Maisie.' Walkman shakes his head. 'You aren't half going to wish you hadn't said that.'

As he speaks, the buzzer signals end of break. He lowers his arm. 'Go on, but you better look behind you every minute from now on, especially after dark. C'mon Fax.'

Two

'Flitcroft Staff Services, Mavis speaking. How may I help you?'

'Fax. Girl at school, Maisie Malin, starts with the pickles tonight, reckons she's not going to pay.'

Mavis sighs. 'How old is this girl?'

'Thirteen.'

'Thirteen. A baby. Couldn't you have handled this without calling in, Fax? It's what we pay you for.'

'Could have, I suppose.'

'Then kindly do so in future. Charles doesn't like his operators phoning the office. Do we know anything useful about this Maisie Malin – something we might use?'

'Her auntie's a line supervisor, got her the job.'

'Perfect. Listen, let Maisie meet the politicians and if that doesn't do it, be the parent calling in. She'll cave in, no danger. All right?'

'Yeah, thanks. 'Bye.'

THREE

Sandy lifts the bike wheel out of its slot, mounts up and pedals hard to catch her best friend, Beryl. The rush is because this is their GCSE year. Tea, masses of homework *and* Fabrications Inc. Too much to cram in really but the dosh has to come from somewhere and pressing pays one seventy-five an hour.

'Hey, Bez – slow down before you gimme heart attack.'

'Can't, Sand. Mum's on lates and I'm getting the tea.'

'What you having?'

'Search me. Whatever she's left out.'

'We're having tuna casserole.'

'Oooh yuck!'

'I know. Can't *stand* tuna. Think I'll tell Mum I ate a big lunch.'

'You *did*.'

'What, that pizza? It was so thin you could read through it. And she shook the scoop so I only got about four chips.'

They reach the T-junction, wait, swing left on Skopje Way. Skopje is Cottoncroft's twin town and this is a busy road – part of the outer ring. The girls live a mile away on the Tree Estate.

'Hey, Sand, you know this whatsit – national minimum wage?'

'Heard of it, yeah.'

'Think it applies to us?'

'Does it *thump*. Wouldn't employ us if it did, would they? What is it – three sixty-five an hour?'

'Be nice though, wouldn't it? Three sixty-five an hour, seventeen-and-a-half hours. That'd be . . . what? Eighty-eight, eighty-nine quid?'

'Less ten per cent to Push.'

'OK – still leave around eighty though, wouldn't it?'

'In your dreams, Bez. I'd be happy with what I get *now* if it wasn't for those Bugsy Malone actalikes. Why should *I* give Charles and Mavis Flitcroft three quid a week when they're rolling in it? Why should *anybody*? We ought to get together and *do* something about it.'

4

'In *your* dreams, Sand. See you at work.' Beryl swerves left on to Alder Drive. Sandy rides on, heading for Poplar Nook and tuna casserole. It is twenty to four.

FOUR

Five past nine. Dark already, with that chill in the air you sometimes get in September. Maisie Malin comes out of Posh Spice Pickles and stands on the step while her smarting eyes adjust. She has spent three hours topping and tailing small onions and is feeling slightly nauseous. She takes deep breaths of the cold clean air. When she exhales she imagines gusts of greenish vapour round her head. Girls and women push past, clattering across the cobbled yard, hurrying away to children, husbands, homework. Auntie Vi emerges, circles Maisie's waist with a thin arm and squeezes. 'All right, love?'

Maisie smiles. 'Yeah. Bit sick. Onions.'

The woman nods. 'It's the fumes. You'll soon get used to it. I don't even notice.'

Maisie grins. 'Smell 'em on you though, Auntie Vi. All the time.'

'Aye, so your uncle's always saying. I tell him,

think about the dosh. See you tomorrow, love.'

Maisie nods, watches her aunt depart. They live in opposite directions. Most of the shift has gone already, swallowed by the dark. Behind her, lights are going out. She crosses the yard and sets off down dingy, narrow Cardigan Street with its dim lamps and run-down, failing mills.

The nausea has passed and Maisie is thinking about the three pounds seventy-five she's earned, when two figures step from the gateway of a derelict factory, forcing her to stop. She recognizes John Major and Tony Blair. They don't speak, but grin inanely at her as she stammers, 'W-what d'you want? I . . . I've only got sixty pence, you can have it only don't hurt me.' She can see eyes glittering through the eyeholes in their masks. Without speaking they dart forward, grab fistfuls of her hair and clothing and wrestle her to the ground. She can't cry out or see what's happening because Major's clamped a hand over her mouth and is sitting astride her chest, but it feels like Blair's undoing her trainers. She writhes and kicks, thinking *they're going to strip me*, but as soon as her shoes are off they get up and walk away as if she doesn't exist, dangling the seventy-quid Nikes by their laces.

She's outraged as much by their coolness as by their assault on her. They're not running. They haven't even glanced back. A part of her wants to pelt after them, grab her trainers and beat them over the head with them so they'll be forced to notice her, but she stays where she is. She's watching seventy quid walk away, but she knows it might have been worse. A lot worse. She sits on the damp flags till the politicians pass from sight round a bend, then gets up and hobbles homeward in her stocking feet, trying not to think how many onions she'll top and tail to make back seventy pounds.

FIVE

Tuesday, ten past nine. Human Biology with Mr Vessels, known as Blood. The teacher's eye falls on a tat-headed lad lolling near the back of the room. 'Have you got something for me, Kieran?'

'Sir.' The boy nods, clambers to his feet, offers a dog-eared folder containing his weekend homework. He should have handed it in yesterday but didn't get it done till last night. Blood handles the folder as if it's been dipped in liquid faeces, drops it on his desk and wipes his hands down the sides of his corduroy trousers. He doesn't care for Kieran Billings, who always looks as though he's been interrogated continuously for seventy-two hours.

'Right.' Vessels rubs his hands together and beams

at the GCSE hopefuls in front of him. 'The lymphatic system.' Billings, in slow motion like a two-toed sloth, subsides into the chair, drapes a limp arm over the back of it and dozes.

Kieran's weekends go like this: Saturday morning, up at four to be at the pick-up point by half-past. Two and a half hours crammed in the back of a bouncing, diesel-reeking van with eleven other kids bound for a farm in Norfolk. Ten hours, seven-fifteen till five-fifteen, standing by a moving belt, chopping and bagging leeks. A scratch meal and a night on a mattress in a sort of barrack hut, followed by another ten-hour shift and the long ride home. Gross pay sixty pounds for the two days, deduct fifteen pounds for transport, two for grub and two for overalls and ten per cent protection, leaving thirty-five pounds clear.

Not a lot of dosh, and not much energy left for homework and the study of the lymphatic system.

SIX

Three-forty. Maisie comes out of school and hurries away, surprised nobody's come on to her for dosh. Her parents don't know she was assaulted and robbed last night. She hasn't told them, because if she did she'd not be working at Posh Spice Pickles tonight or any other night, and how would she replace her Nikes then? She hasn't told them about the Nikes either, hoping that by the time they ask she'll have dreamed up a convincing story.

She knows whose faces last night's masks concealed but she has no proof, and without it there's no point going to a teacher. Barraclough and Longstaff are fifteen. They've been Push for two years but nobody'd know it. They take care never to be in trouble at school. If she were to accuse them of stealing her trainers she'd be in bother, not them.

She turns the corner on to Skopje Way and practically bumps into Malcolm Longstaff. 'Whoops-a-daisy, Maisie.' He grins like a wolf. 'I *told* you you'd have to watch your step from now on, didn't I?'

Maisie draws back. 'What d'you want?' Kids are passing but none of them looks at Longstaff or Maisie. Push business is Push business.

'Me? I don't want *anything*, Maisie, unless there's something you'd like to give me. Is there?'

'I know it was you last night. You and Barraclough. What you done with my trainers?'

'Sorry?'

'Don't pretend you don't know what I'm on about. Cardigan Street. The masks.'

'Huh?' The boy shakes his head. 'You're barmy, kiddo. *Is* there something you want to give me?'

9

'Oh yes, there's something I want to give you all right and you'll get it too, sooner or later.'

'You mean the one eighty-eight you owe us?'

'No I don't.'

'Pity. I felt sure you'd be ready to buy into the service we offer, especially if you've had a spot of bother with guys in masks. Specialize in seeing their sort off, we do. Still –' he shrugs – 'you can always change your mind later. Be good.'

He steps aside and Maisie hurries on.

SEVEN

Wednesday morning, ten to nine. Golden mist veils the rising sun but it's going to be warm later on. Sandy parks her bike, tells Beryl she'll see her in a bit, and crosses to the science block where some Pakistani boys are leaning against the wall, chatting. She zeros in on Shazad Butt whose sister, Sushila, is a friend. 'Got a minute, Shaz?'

'Oooh, hear *that*, lads?' The boys grin, nudge one another. 'Got a minute, Shaz. Something going on we should know about or what?'

'Shut up, you turkeys.' Butt scowls at Sandy. 'What's it about?'

'That's what we *all* want to know,' laughs Shofiq Ali.

'Work.' Sandy feels her cheeks flare. 'It's about work.'

'I don't get it, but OK.' He detaches himself from the wall and falls in beside her, hands in pockets as she moves away. Somebody calls after them, 'Send us an invite to the wedding, eh, Shaz?' Sandy heads for the playing field where there's less chance of being overheard.

'Sushila says you work in your dad's restaurant.'

'Yes, what about it?'

'I don't mean to be cheeky, but do you get paid?'

'Ha!' The boy decapitates a dandelion clock with a vicious kick. 'If you call a quid an hour getting paid, yes I do.'

She glances sidelong at him. 'Quid, is that all? *I* get one seventy-five.'

'You're not working for your family.' He smiles tightly. 'It's not so much a job as a duty, see? My dad and my uncles could make me work for nothing if they wanted. The quid an hour's sort of a favour.'

'Some favour. And those guys back there – your mates – do most of them have jobs?'

'Oh yeah, but they don't all work for their families. Some are on two, two-fifty an hour, *and* they only do about ten hours to my fifty-six and a half.'

'You work *fifty-six and a half hours a week*?'

'Yeah, that's how come I yawn all day and don't hand in homework.'

'That's . . . awful, I'd no idea. So you get fifty-six quid a week?'

''S right.' He grins. 'Saving up for my first Porsche.' He looks at her, frowns. 'Why are you interested in all this, Sandy — is it a flipping *survey* or what?'

'No it's not a survey, Shaz, it's about Push. You don't pay 'em, do you? Not just you, *none* of the Pakistanis pay, is that right?'

'You *bet* we don't. It doesn't come easy enough to give it away to bandits.'

'Yeah, I know, but *how* don't you pay? I mean, how come none of you gets beaten up or anything?'

'Ah.' Again the tight smile. 'That's easy. Push is an organization, right? One that's prepared to use violence.'

Sandy pulls a face. 'You got that one right.'

'Well we — I mean our *community* — has its own organizations.' He shakes his head. 'They're not violent in the normal course of events, but certain ones will *resort* to violence if that becomes necessary — if our people are threatened.' He shrugs. 'Froggy Flitcroft knows this and leaves us alone.'

'Hmmm.' Sandy scowls at the dewy grass. 'So that's what it takes — an organization.' She smiles at him. 'Thanks, Shaz.'

'You're welcome, but wha —?'

'Can't say, Shaz. Not yet.' As she walks away, the sun breaks through the mist.

EIGHT

Eight o'clock. It's been a warm day but the sun set some time ago, especially on Back Quebec Street. There's a chill in the air. Six young Push operatives sit on saggy bits of ruined furniture in the half-light of a dank chamber with walls of crumbling brick and a stone floor. Built as a stable towards the end of the nineteenth century, it has had many uses in the twentieth and will be obliterated in the early years of the twenty-first. But for now it belongs to Charles and Mavis Flitcroft of Flitcroft Staff Services, whose smart office on Manchester Road is connected to it by a dim, narrow passageway.

'How are you at getting up in the morning, Cassette?'

'Average,' says the girl. 'Why?'

Fax smiles nastily. 'Dirty little job for you tomorrow.'

'Tomorrow's Thursday. School.'

'This is *before* school, dummy. Well before. Five a.m. to be exact.'

'Why me?'

''Cause you're new and the new guy always gets the dirty job.'

'OK, what d'you want me to do?'

'You know the newsagent on the corner of Long Lane and Gas Street – Patel's?'

Cassette nods. Her real name is Anne Myers. She prefers Cassette.

'Van drops the morning papers in the doorway just before five. Three bundles. The Patels live above the shop. He gets up at five-thirty, carries the bundles inside to sort for delivery. When he picks 'em up tomorrow they won't be fit to sort *or* deliver. You'll have seen to that.'

'How?'

'Poo sticks.'

'What d'you mean?'

'What d'you *mean* what do I mean? Surely you know about poo sticks?' A ripple of mirth in the gloom. Cassette shakes her head.

'OK, listen. These bundles of papers are bound up really tight. They won't catch fire, and if you pour stuff over them – paint, say – it only reaches a few. So what we do is we get a bucket, half-fill it with dog muck, which isn't hard 'cause Cottoncroft's the dog-muck capital of the world, add water, and stir briskly till we have a thickish batter. Only other thing we need's lots and lots of lolly sticks. You know –

those flat sticks you're left with when your ice lolly's all gone? Now we don't have your actual lolly sticks but what we *do* have is a generous supply of those things doctors hold your tongue down with and tell you to say "aaah". Spatulas. These spatulas are your poo sticks. What we do is, we drop a few handfuls in the bucket and give it a good swill round. This coats the sticks with our batter, so we *don't* stick 'em in our gob and say "aaah". What we do, as we squat in Patel's doorway being very, very quiet, is fish out the sticks one by one and slide 'em in between the papers. If we've any sense we wear rubber gloves, and we don't have a big breakfast before we set off. We needn't shove our sticks between *every* paper 'cause that'd take too long. Every third paper will do. There'll be nobody about, and if you work fast you'll be done and away in ten minutes. Any questions?'

'Yeah.' The girl looks ill. 'Do I have to?'

Fax gazes at her. 'D'you like the little wraps?'

'You know I do.'

'Well, there you go. Anything else?'

'Uh-huh. What's Patel done?'

'Patel? He has twelve paper girls. Five in the morning, four in the evening, three on Sundays, and not one of 'em pays. Not one. He's been warned but he takes no notice.' The boy grins. 'I bet he takes notice tomorrow.'

NINE

Thursday, seven a.m. Jill Hall strides grinning into the shop. She's a star – always first, always cheerful. 'Morning, Mr Patel. Bit nippy.'

'Nippy, yes.' He's not his usual self. Jill looks at him.

'Nothing wrong, is there?' Occasionally there's a complaint from a customer. *Tell that girl not to leave my paper sticking out of the slot: it's like papier mâché when it rains.* Patel nods.

'Something is *very* wrong, Jill. Look.' He takes papers from under the counter, fans them out. 'Some dirty filthy person has done this to all my papers. It is doggy poo.'

'Doggy poo?' Jill wrinkles up her nose.

'Yes, I think so. There was this note.' He passes a scrap of paper to the girl.

Dogged by bad luck eh, Patel? You were warned.

She frowns, handing it back. 'What do they mean, warned? Warned by who?'

Patel pulls a face. 'I think it is because you and the others do not pay Push money. I'm afraid I must ask you all to begin paying before you do your rounds again.'

'What – this *morning*?'

'Oh, no, Jill – there will be no deliveries this morning. I'm sorry, and of course I will pay you all because it's my fault.'

'It is *not!*' explodes Jill. 'It's Push's fault. *They* put the dog-dirt on your papers. People like that deserve to be locked up.'

'Ah, but they won't be, Jill, because everybody is afraid. *I* am afraid. If I were Pakistani there are organizations I could call on for protection, but we Indians have nothing like that in Cottoncroft. So, as soon as I've explained to the others what has happened I must phone my supplier, ask do I return these filthy papers or throw them away. And all of you girls must pay the ten per cent from now on. If you do not, then believe me, worse things will follow.' He shakes his head. 'Who knows what might happen to a young girl doing her round on a dark winter morning, a dark winter evening? And it will soon be winter.'

TEN

'*You're* back early, love. *Jog* round, did you?' Catherine Hall, in dressing gown and slippers, is setting the table for breakfast. It is a quarter past seven. Her daughter shakes her head.

'No papers today, Mum. Somebody smeared dog muck on 'em so Mr Patel sent us home.'

'Dog muck?' Her mother pulls a face. 'Because he's Pakistani, I suppose.'

'No, Mum, he says it's because we haven't been paying Push dosh – and he isn't Pakistani, he's Indian.'

'Ah!' She fills the kettle, places it on its base. 'Those Flitcrofts are a blight on this town. It's a disgrace how they get away with it year after year when everybody knows what they do.'

'How *do* they get away with it, Mum? You'd think the police –'

'Oh, they've been investigated, love, more than once, but there's never enough evidence. They run a legitimate business and use other people to do their dirty work. They know exactly what they're doing. I keep telling myself they'll come unstuck one of these days, but it's taking a heck of a long time.' She snorts. 'Whoever it was said crime doesn't pay can't have seen Mavis Flitcroft cruising about in that white Mercedes of hers. D'you want toast, love, or are you sticking to cornflakes?'

By half eight Jill is in the schoolyard. Penny Cockroft and Jane Tillotson are there too. 'Feels funny, doesn't it?' says Jane. 'All this time in a morning. What did we do before we got paper rounds?'

'*I* laid in bed,' growls Penny, 'and I would have this morning if I'd known.'

'Yes, but what did we do without the *dosh*?' asks Jill.

Jane frowns. 'Good question. Trouble is, we'll have to do without some of it from now on 'cause we'll be paying Push – *I* will anyway.'

'Me too,' mumbles Jill. 'Worse luck. How about you, Pen?'

'I suppose. We'd better tell Claire and Nikki when they get here too.' Claire and Nikki are twins.

'I wish we had a gang,' murmurs Jill, 'like Push, only bigger and harder. We wouldn't have to pay ten per cent *then*.'

'Hey.' Penny looked at her friends. 'Why don't we *start* a gang? A gang of kids who've got jobs?' Her eyes shine. 'Think about it. Some of 'em would be fifteen, sixteen. There'd be boys. We could –'

'Oh sure!' scoffs Jane. 'See fifteen-year-old lads standing in line to join a gang run by thirteen-year-old girls. Happens all the time.'

'I don't mean run it. I didn't say *run*. We could mention it as an idea, that's all, see if anyone's interested.'

Jane gazes at her. 'Yeah, like *who* for instance? Who do we mention it *to*, Pen? Josh Winnifrith, the Schwarzenegger of Year Eleven? He'd rip your head off and pull your lungs out through your neck.'

'I know someone we could mention it to,' says Jill.

'Yeah, who?'

'Sandra Lister.'

'Why her?'

''Cause I was talking to Maisie Malin and she told me she was passing Sandra and a friend in the yard, and she heard Sandra muttering about Push, saying something ought to be done. Sandra's got a job at Fabrications Inc. I don't mind mentioning your idea to her, Penny.'

'Well, you could do it right now,' growls Jane. 'She's just ridden through the gateway with her side-kick, Cawthra.'

'Yes, OK.' Jill moves towards the bike sheds as the two older girls dismount. Jane and Penny watch from a distance, half-expecting their friend to be driven away for daring to address a Year Eleven in public.

ELEVEN

'Patel Newsagents, Anwar Patel speaking.'

'Oh, Mr Patel, this is Mrs Gudgeon at forty Mint Street. I'm calling because we didn't get our paper this morning, or next week's *Radio Times*. Did the girl let you down or something?'

'No, Mrs Gudgeon, it wasn't that. Somebody vandalized my papers early this morning so I wasn't able to send any of my girls round. I'm in the process of phoning my customers but it's a slow job because they keep phoning *me*.'

'Oh, I'm sorry – I'll get off the line.'

'No, no, no, Mrs Gudgeon, I didn't mean *that*. I'm not criticizing those who are phoning me: I'd do the same in their place. I was merely explaining why you've *had* to phone. Everything will be back to normal tomorrow, your *Radio Times* will come with tomorrow's paper and, of course, the price of today's will be deducted from your bill. I'm truly sorry about this, and I assure you nothing of the sort will happen again.'

'Thank you, Mr Patel, and I'm sorry for your troubles. Goodbye.'

'Hello . . . is that the paper shop?'

'Yes, this is Patels, Anwar Pa –'

'What the *hell* happened to my paper this morning, Patel, and how come your blasted phone's engaged all the time? Jabbering to Bombay, were you?'

'No, no, Mr . . . who *is* calling, please?'

'Who is calling? *I'm* calling. *Me*. The one whose paper's always left sticking out the slot when it rains. The one who pays you nine quid a week for papier mâché. Or *did*, I should say. Not any more.'

'Ah – it is Mr Jordan, yes? I was about to call you, Mr Jordan, to explain – '

'I'm not interested in your explanations, sunshine. You've been flamin' useless all the time you've had my order and now you can cancel it, and don't think I'm paying for the three rags I've had this week either: I'm keeping that money as compensation for the inconvenience I've suffered. I'm taking my custom to Mitchell's on Lofthouse Road because *they* deliver papers in a readable condition, and if I read one day that you've packed up and gone back to Uttar Pradesh or wherever it is you came from, I'll be a happy man.'

'Goodbye then, Mr Jordan. Nice to have done business with you . . .'

TWELVE

'So what's the news?' asks Jane. 'Did Sandra go for Pen's brilliant idea?'

Jill shrugs. 'I wouldn't say *go for*, exactly, but she's thinking about it. Said a similar idea had already crossed *her* mind, but I think she said that so she doesn't have to tell people it came from some squirt in Year Nine. Reckons if she can get a few Year Elevens interested it might take off.' Jill grins. 'So,

Charles and Mavis could be in for a bit of a shock before long.'

'Ooh, I don't half *hope* so,' murmurs Penny. 'Why the heck should I drag myself out of bed at six o'clock on a freezing January morning so Mavis Flitcroft can turn over and sleep till nine?'

Jill shakes her head. 'No reason at all, Pen. On the other hand,' she grins, 'you could try telling yourself it's better to be out of your bed than in hers, 'cause she'll have Charles sprawled next to her with that slitty mouth and big freckled hands, like sleeping with a dead frog.'

THIRTEEN

Morning break. Sandy and Beryl by the bike sheds. Beryl looks at Sandy. 'So what did he say?'

'Gary?' Sandy shrugs. 'Says he'll pass it on, but doubts if anyone'll be keen to cross Push.'

'That's what *I* said. Better to have ninety per cent of your wage and be fit than no job and a gap where your front teeth used to be.'

'Those Year Nine girls don't feel that way, Bez. Raring to go, they are.'

'So?' Beryl frowns. 'That makes six of you, Sand.

Five thirteen-year-olds and yourself. Can't see Push fainting with terror over *that* army. And, as for the Flitcrofts, they'll just make sure none of you works in Cottoncroft again.'

Sandy gazes at her friend. 'Remember when we did the Nazis with old Distant?' Distant was what the kids called Mr Pasternak, the head of History.

'Yeah, what's *that* got to do with anything?'

'How many members did the Nazi party have in nineteen-twenty?'

'God, Sand – *I* don't know. How many?'

'I don't remember exactly but I think it was ten. People laughed at 'em on the street. Thirteen years later they took over Germany.'

'They had *Hitler*, Sand. You're no Hitler, you haven't got thirteen years and even *he* couldn't have got started with a handful of Year Nines.' She shakes her head. 'It'll never get off the ground.'

Sandy shrugs. 'You could be right. Just have to wait and see, won't we?'

FOURTEEN

'Hey, Kieran, got a minute?' Afternoon break. Gary Waterhouse is leaning against the gardener's shed, dipping into a bag of crisps. Kieran Billings saunters across. 'What?'

'You do a job don't you, weekends?'

'Uh-huh. Why?'

'Some of us're getting ballsed off with Push, think it's time we stood up to 'em over this ten per cent scam. What d'you reckon?'

The boy shrugs. 'Maybe, but I'm on the veg where the main problem's the Gangmasters. They rip us off a lot worse than Push.'

'What the heck's a Gangmaster?'

'You know – guy cuts a deal with some farmer to supply temporary labour at so much an hour per man. Three quid, say. He recruits guys, delivers 'em to the farm. The farmer pays him three quid an hour for each man, but he gives the guys two quid and pockets the rest. *And* he docks us extra for petrol and overalls. They're nothing but a bunch of crooks, Gangmasters.'

'Ah, well.' Gary offers the packet. 'Nothing we can do about *them*, but ten per cent's ten per cent. Better in your pocket than Flitcroft's.'

'True.' Kieran takes a crisp. 'Question is, how do we stand up to 'em? Push don't screw around, Gaz. Break your legs as soon as look at you.'

'Hundreds of kids work in this town, Kieran. The Push can't break *all* their legs.'

'No, but they can break *mine*, and that's what every

kid'll think who's asked to stop paying his dues. They're *scared*, Gaz.'

'Yeah, I know.' Gary upends the bag over his open mouth to get the crumbs, balls up the bag and shoves it in his pocket. 'We need to show that the Push aren't as hard as everybody *thinks* they are.'

'But they *are* as hard as everybody thinks they are.'

'Not the ones in school – Barraclough and them.'

'So what're you suggesting?'

'I'm suggesting getting 'em one at a time and beating the living daylights out of them. Don't tell me *you* couldn't take Gordon Barraclough, for instance.'

'Sure I could, but then three of his mates'd ambush me one night and put me in hospital.'

'Not if he didn't know who hit him.'

'Oh yeah, and how'd I manage *that* – make myself invisible or something?'

'You could wear a mask, Kieran. It's what *they* do.'

Kieran sighs. 'OK, so I wear a mask and beat the bejesus out of Gordon Barraclough. What good does it do?'

'It demonstrates that a guy's not unassailable just 'cause he's Push. It says *look – whack this guy across the kisser with a length of four-by-two and he bruises like anybody else.* It's a process of de-mythologization.'

'Is *that* what it is?' Kieran chuckles. 'Tell you what then, Gary: I'll watch while *you* de-mythologize a couple of these guys, and if you're still healthy three weeks later I'll have a go.'

'D'you promise?'

'Sure, if I don't get pulverized in a van smash on the way to some soggy farm in Norfolk one Saturday morning. See you later.'

'Yeah, Kieran. Later.'

FIFTEEN

Friday morning. 'Dorothy.' Mr Dick swoops on the thicky of Year Ten. 'Last week we decided that many nineteenth-century novelists made use of the Pathetic Fallacy in their writings. Tell us what is meant by the Pathetic Fallacy.'

Dorothy Comstock stares at the folder in her lap. 'Er – well, like . . .' She hates English. Hates *school*. She can feel Moby's eyes like lasers, burning twin holes through the top of her skull. She doesn't know what he's talking about, he *knows* she doesn't know, and she knows he knows she doesn't know. It's a game he plays with her because she's what he likes to refer to as a *muppet*; a Year Ten who'll never make it to Year Eleven because she's destined to fail GCSE in all subjects.

'You don't *know*, do you, Dorothy?' The teacher's tone drips sarcasm. 'But of *course* you don't. After all it's been a whole week since we talked about it, and a week's a long time to a muppet. *What* sort of creature finds a week a long time, Dorothy?'

'Sir, a muppet, sir.'

'That's *right*, Dorothy.' Mr Dick smiles but he's puzzled. He's good at this, he knows it, and he can't understand why the kids aren't sniggering behind their hands. All pupils like to see one of their number squirm: he'd have had most classes in tucks by now.

What Mr Dick doesn't know is that Dorothy Comstock has another name. A night-time name. The one she's known by in Push. Dot Com they call her, and nobody sniggers behind their hands at her. *Nobody.* Everyone's good at something, and Dorothy's special talents sleep till sunset, like vampires. Moby Dick doesn't know it but he's crossed an invisible line today: the line between what Dot Com is prepared to put up with and what she isn't. By crossing the line he has earned himself a demonstration of Dot Com's particular expertise. It won't be long in coming, he won't know who it's from and he certainly won't enjoy it. But then if you can't take it, you shouldn't dish it out.

SIXTEEN

'Now then, love – what d'you think, now you've done a week?' Auntie Vi takes down her coat, hangs up her overall. Maisie smiles. Her eyes still smart, but not like Monday.

'It's fine, Auntie Vi.'

'You'll stick it then?'

'Oh yes, I think so.'

'*This* feels nice, doesn't it?' The woman is stowing her wages in her bag.

'Yeah.' Maisie pats her pocket. 'Eighteen seventy-five.' *Minus one eighty-eight for Push*, she thinks but doesn't say. *Leaving sixteen eighty-seven. Four and a bit weeks to pay for those flipping trainers.*

'Listen, love.' Her aunt speaks very softly. 'Be careful who you talk to about your job. You're not supposed to work after seven at night at your age. If the wrong person finds out, all the kids lose their jobs and Mr Snowden gets fined. OK?'

'Sure.'

'Good girl. 'Night.'

Maisie doesn't fancy Cardigan Street by herself so she does what she's done since Tuesday, hurrying to stay close behind three women who walk the same route. Husbands and fathers collect most of the shift with their cars but of these three, two are divorced and the other is a widow. Their journey home is lightened by lively chat and they'd be happy to have Maisie walk with them, but they haven't noticed her and she's too shy just to tag along.

Not that Push're going to bother me, she tells herself for the fiftieth time, *now that I'm paying. Why should they?* All the same, Cardigan Street is creepy at this time of night and Maisie trots to keep the three within shouting distance.

SEVENTEEN

Thirlmere Park is a nice neighbourhood. Four-bedroom detached houses with spacious gardens and gravelled driveways giving on to wide, tree-lined avenues. The park at the centre of the complex contains an ornamental lake with fountains, islets and exotic waterfowl. Nobody throws styrofoam burger trays into the water. Nobody stones the birds. The many abstract sculptures for which the park is famous are devoid of spraycan art. No litter accumulates on the softly undulating expanses of manicured grass, and no homeless persons doss down in its wrought-iron gazebos. Thirlmere Park is a prosperous place and a Neighbourhood Watch area, and most residents know of at least one neighbour who seems to do little else but watch. In short, the dominant feeling in Thirlmere Park is one of security, and it isn't surprising therefore that Monica and Edward Dick are pretty relaxed about letting their infant daughter ride her trike up and down their drive, provided she doesn't go through the gateway.

Dorothy Comstock sticks out in this neighbourhood like a turd in a punchbowl and she knows it. She doesn't loiter this fine Saturday morning because she doesn't need to. She's done her homework. Knows which house the Dicks occupy, and all about little Dorrit's trike rides. She's passing the place for only the second time when the dungareed infant comes pumping down the driveway, executes a neat u-turn and sets off back.

'Hello, Dorrit.' The child stops pedalling, twists round to see who spoke. Dorothy nods at the scarlet trike. 'Nice rig.'

Dorrit scowls. *Who's this? How does she know my name?*

'Birthday present, was it?'

The infant shakes her head, mumbles, 'No, Daddy got it for me.' She's trying to remember something Mummy said about talking to people. People we don't know, but this lady knows her. Knows her name.

'D'you know what'd look good on you, Dorrit, really, *really* cool when you're riding your trike?'

Dorrit doesn't understand, hasn't encountered cool, but recognizes a question. She shakes her head.

'A crash helmet. You know.' The lady's hands make smoothing movements round her own head. 'Like bikers wear. Grown-up bikers.'

Dorrit knows vaguely what Dorothy's describing. Big shiny hats with glass to look through. And she certainly knows grown up. Grown up's good. She grins, which seems to please the lady.

'Would you *like* a crash helmet, Dorrit? I know where there is one. Make you look *really* grown up.'

Dorrit grins, nods. 'Yes, please.'

'Come on then – it's just round the corner.'

'Mummy says I'm never to go out there.'

Dorothy chuckles. 'She means by *yourself*, Dorrit. I'm with you now, I'll look after you. Come on.'

Dense cypress hedges set to screen the houses from the road ensure there is no witness, even here. Sixty seconds after passing through her own gateway, Dorrit is gone. The red trike stands in a stripe of sunlight where Monica Dick will find it, and scream.

EIGHTEEN

Saturday, eight o'clock. A dark, cold evening with a sneaky wind. Not unusual for late September. What *might* strike a casual observer as odd is the number of people turning into Back Quebec Street, a narrow, unlighted alleyway curving round the back of the Odeon cinema to connect Quebec Street with Manchester Road. There's little action in Back Quebec Street even in the daytime: bollards across its mouth prevent vehicles using it as a rat-run, and the businesses whose mouldering premises scowl at each other across its greasy cobbles either dwindled to nothing long ago or relocated. Nowadays the Odeon's three wheely-bins have the place to themselves, except on Thursday mornings when loud men in Doc Martens trundle them out on to Manchester Road where the refuse truck stands grumbling.

Halfway along Back Quebec Street, on the left if you're coming from the Quebec Street end, there's a pair of big wooden doors in an otherwise featureless brick wall. These doors were swung shut and bolted sometime in the fifties and haven't been opened since. Beyond the doors lies a dank yard and a clutch of crumbling buildings. This is Push Headquarters: what Charles Flitcroft likes to think of as the operational nerve-centre of his business empire. If wheely-bins had eyes, the Odeon trio would be entertained most evenings by the furtive coming and going of Flitcroft's shady employees, some of them surprisingly young. They do not enter and leave through Flitcroft Staff Services, but by way of a little door set in one of the big doors on Back Quebec Street. No light spills out when this door is opened, and it never stays open long.

'Anyone seen Dot Com?' Sparky Sparks turns from the table with Dorothy's consignment of wraps in his meaty paws. Her failure to step up and take them constitutes a glitch in an otherwise smooth oper-ation, and Sparky doesn't like glitches. His eyes pene-trate the gloom and fix on Lois Baxter's bulky shape. 'What about you, Email?' Email is Lois's Push handle, the kids call her Email the female. She shakes her head.

'Haven't seen her, Sparky. Maybe she's sick.'

'She'll be a damn sight sicker next time I see her. Here, you'll have to make her connections after your own. Fax'll help you.'

'Aw, *Sparky*. What about my homework?'

He scowls at her. 'Fancy doing your homework with all your fingers broke?'

'Oh, sure.' Lois accepts the extra wraps, slips them

34

into a pocket thinking, *it'll be eleven before I get home. Thank God tomorrow's Sunday.*

Email flits across the yard, exits through the little door which Colin Day closes behind her. Fax follows a minute later, then Cassette, then one of the older distributors. Within an hour Sparky's table is clear. Distributors have set off in every direction, bent on bringing relief to the twitchy punters who loiter on corners in every part of Cottoncroft, waiting with dry throats and runny noses for their little packs of powdered happiness. When Sparky bolts the door and lets himself out through his boss's office, Dorothy still hasn't shown up. As for the boss himself, he's far too smart to visit Back Quebec Street when they're dishing out the stuff. That's why he's the boss.

NINETEEN

Ten o'clock, and it's been a really bad day for the Dicks. Twelve hours have passed since Monica went to check up on Dorrit and found the little red trike. The police were called at once, and were most reassuring. 'She's probably playing on a bit of grass somewhere, perfectly happy. We see it all the time.'

Sounded feasible at five past ten this morning, rather

less so at midday, and when dusk set in around seven-thirty it lost the last of its capacity to comfort. Monica broke down then and the police had to get a doctor to administer a sedative. Now she lies curled on the sofa with a balled-up hanky to her mouth, while Edward sits cross-legged on the rug, holding her hand. They've both spent the day tramping the neighbourhood and beyond, calling their daughter's name. Edward has been out with the car too, cruising the streets of Cottoncroft, and of course they've phoned every home they can think of where the child might conceivably be. Monica now believes that Dorrit is dead. Only the drug keeps her from screaming and screaming. Edward stares at the phone, willing somebody to call with a ransom demand. At the same time a part of his brain scans a list of acquaintances, any one of whom might have harboured and finally succumbed to an unclean urge in respect of the three-year-old. Their milkman. The guy down the sweetshop. That postman with the funny eye. He is appalled by the realization that it might be anybody. Anybody.

It is ten past ten when the phone rings. A policewoman is nearest and picks up. The Dicks, nerves stretched to snapping point, stare at her as she listens, speaks. 'Yes it is. Yes. Right.' Their hearts kick as she turns to them, nodding, cracking a smile. 'That's terrific. Yes, thanks. 'Bye.'

'She's safe and well. A security guard heard someone crying in the ladies' lavatory at the Lazenby Mall. It was coming from a locked cubicle. He kicked the lock off and there was Dorrit, sitting on the seat, cuddling her Kermit.'

'Thank God – oh, thank God!' Monica is on her feet, adrenaline swamping the sedative. Edward is up too. The couple cling together in the middle of the room, weeping. The policewoman, very young, feels happy and embarrassed at the same time. She wonders whether she ought to slip out of the room, give them some privacy. She has just decided to do this when Edward lifts his wet face from his wife's shoulder and croaks, '*What* Kermit? She hasn't *got* a Kermit.'

TWENTY

Monday morning. Edward Dick steers the Volvo through the gateway, slows as a young cyclist swerves across his path. A knot of pupils watch from the doorway of the terrapin as the car crosses the yard and scrunches to a stop in its space under the windows of the science block. The teacher gets out, reaches back in for his briefcase. His movements are those of a tired man, as though the weekend has failed to revive him.

The Volvo's hazard lights flash briefly as he arms the alarm, then he is walking towards the staff entrance. He notices that some pupils by the terrapin are watching him, and that Dorothy Comstock is one of them. The sight of her sends a wave of nausea through him. Dorothy's pudding face has haunted his dreams for the past two nights, alternating with the inanely grinning face of a jokey green frog. She's Moby's prime suspect, though it's hard for him to imagine her having either the intelligence or the imagination to plot a revenge so refined in its cruelty. He'd dearly love to get Dorothy by herself and beat the truth out of her, but of course he can't. The fact that he's frequently called the girl a Muppet and that Kermit is a Muppet is conclusive evidence as far as he's concerned, but would look like coincidence to anybody else. He hasn't even murmured her name to the police.

As Dick reaches for the door handle a touch on his shoulder makes him turn. Dorothy has intercepted him and is gazing into his eyes, saying something. He watches her lips, fighting an urge to lash out.

'Mr Dick. Some of us want you to know how glad we are that your little girl turned up safe and sound. We heard it yesterday on radio, how she was missing for twelve hours. *Twelve hours.*' She shakes her head. 'Must've felt like a *lifetime* to you and Mrs Dick. You know – like a week does to a muppet.'

TWENTY-ONE

Monday lunch. Somebody's pinned a notice on the board between the changing-room doors. The board is for sport-related notices. This one breaks the convention.

DOSH! DOSH! DOSH!
Meeting 3.30 Monday Year 12 common room.
Subject: Push dosh and how not to pay.
All working kids welcome.

It is a well-timed notice, because every working pupil in school has been relieved of ten per cent of his wages since half-eight this morning. At ten to one it catches the eye of Anne Myers, alias Cassette. She rips it down and stuffs it in her pocket to show the others, but by then it has been seen by quite a few kids. When Cassette and her friends turn up at three-thirty to dissuade people from going in, they find Josh Winnifrith on the door and a worrying press of bodies beyond it. They stage a strategic withdrawal.

'OK.' John Passmore stands facing the four semicircles of seated kids and waits for the hubbub to die down. John is an A level student and part-time packer at Bloch Pharmaceuticals. He has agreed to chair the meeting.

'As some of you know, there are people at this school who are sick and tired of shelling out ten per cent of their hard-earned dosh every week to Charles and Mavis Flitcroft, via Push.'

'We *all* are,' cries a voice, and there is a rumble of assent. Passmore nods. 'What the Flitcrofts are doing is illegal, of course. Trouble is, they're too clever to get caught. Everything's done through Push, and there's nothing solid linking Push to Flitcroft Staff Services. From the outside it looks like the sort of protection racket you get in schools everywhere: a gang of bullies extracting kids' lunch-money through terror. The whole *town* knows it's more than that, but there's never any proof.'

'We *know* all this,' growls Beryl Cawthra. 'The point is, what do we *do* about it?'

The boy nods again. 'I'm coming to that now. The situation boils down to this: the Flitcrofts are totally dependant on Push collecting their cut. No Push, no cut. So. The way not to pay is to get rid of Push.'

'Brilliant!' Beryl's voice drips sarcasm. 'You don't need an A-level brain to work that out, John. We *all* know that. It's the *how* that needs a stroke of genius. *How* to get rid of Push.'

Passmore smiles patiently. 'I'm coming to that too,

Beryl, and this *isn't* from my A-level brain. It's what some people in this room have worked out. Actually, getting rid of Push will be dead easy . . .'

'Oh, yeah!' This from Kieran Billings. 'That's why they've been shoving everybody around for the last ten years is it – 'cause they're dead easy to get rid of?'

'You didn't let me finish. What I was about to say was, getting rid of Push will be dead easy *if we all stick together.*'

'Oh, right.' Kieran chuckled. 'So *that*'s what we've been doing wrong, eh? Not sticking together.'

'Exactly, Kieran.' He gazes at the boy. 'You're with Selwyn Pogson, aren't you? The Gangmaster?'

'Yeah, so?'

'And like all Gangmasters he rips you off, right?'

'Well, yeah.'

'And you let him because you know what'd happen if you complained.'

'I suppose.'

'What *would* happen, Kieran?'

The boy snorts. 'He'd sack me, of course.'

'But – who'd he find to do your *work*?'

'You're joking – there's a hundred kids waiting to take my place. It'd take him about three seconds to replace me.'

'But what if those hundred kids said no – *we're* not taking Kieran's job, he's our mate?'

'Ah but they wouldn't, would they? They need the dosh.'

Passmore nods. 'And that's why you all work for peanuts, Kieran. Because you're not together.'

'Gaah!' Kieran shakes his head. 'It's easy to talk, John, but it's not that simple. When it comes to it people look out for number one.'

'And that's where Pull's going to be different, Kieran. We'll look out for each *other*.'

'Pull?' Kieran looks blank. 'What you on about, John? What's Pull?'

Passmore grins. 'Pull's the name of an organization, Kieran. An organization that starts here, in this room, today. Pull's the weapon that's going to break the Push. Listen.'

TWENTY-TWO

'Come.' Charles Tate always says 'come' instead of 'come in'. It sounds economical, and economy is a splendid thing in a headmaster. 'Yes, Edward?'

'I wonder if I might have a word with you, Head-master – a personal matter?' The kids call him Hezzy, but it's a good move to call him Headmaster if you want something from him.

'Yes of course, Edward. Take a pew. How *is* your little girl? None the worse for her ordeal, I hope.'

'To be perfectly honest I don't think Dorrit's aware she's *been* through an ordeal, Headmaster. I mean, she wasn't interfered with or anything; they examined her for that. As far as she's concerned a lady took her for a walk, gave her a cuddly toy and went away. She only became distressed when she realized nobody was coming to collect her. It's Monica I worry about. This thing's affected *her* more than Dorrit.'

The Headmaster nods. 'Understandable, Edward. Must've shaken *you* up too though, didn't it? Matter of fact I wasn't expecting you in this morning. Thought you'd need a couple of days to – you know – be with your daughter. Put it behind you.'

Moby shakes his head. 'I'm all right. I'd be coping if it weren't for . . . well, the matter I wanted to talk to you about.'

Tate nods again, settles back in the swivel chair. 'Of course, Edward. Fire away.'

Dick stares at the leather desktop, shakes his head. 'It's . . . difficult, Headmaster. A delicate matter, involving a pupil.'

'Oh, yes?' Tate's eyebrows rise. 'What pupil, Edward?'

'Dorothy Comstock. Year Ten.'

'Yes, I know Dorothy. Is she in trouble?'

'She's . . .' The teacher starts to respond, checks

himself, sighs. 'I've got absolutely no proof in support of what I'm about to say, Headmaster. It's all circumstantial.'

Tate leans forward. 'Go on.'

'I believe it was Dorothy Comstock who abducted my daughter.'

'Good grief!' The Headmaster falls back, stares at Dick. 'This is an extremely serious allegation, Edward. What on earth makes you . . . ?'

Dick, his gaze fixed on the desktop, speaks rapidly. Confesses his dislike of the Comstock girl, his practice of picking on her, the word he uses to belittle her. Muppet. He looks up. 'When my daughter was found she was hugging a soft toy – a frog known as Kermit. Kermit is one of the Muppets, and her abductor must have given it to her.' He goes on to describe the incident in the yard this morning. How Dorothy's sympathetic words were mocked by the malicious gleam in her eye. The thinly veiled reference to his latest sarcastic attack on her. 'All circumstantial I know, Headmaster, but add to it the fact that the girl's a bully – a known member of the gang they call Push, and circumstantial evidence becomes pretty strong. Fact is, I can't see myself teaching a group that includes this girl. Not now. Not after what she's put my family through, and anyway I think it's about time the school took some sort of action over this gang thing.' He gazes at the Headmaster. 'What do *you* think?'

TWENTY-THREE

'Not so fast, Cockroft.' Penny is alone in the cloak-room and halfway into her jacket when the three girls emerge from the toilet cubicle. They are Year Eleven, and they are Push. Penny's heart lurches. 'I've got to go, my dad's waiting with the car.'

Lois Baxter snorts. 'Don't give us that, Cockroft. Your dad doesn't pick you up.' She positions herself by the door so there's no escape. Anne Myers creeps up behind Penny, grabs her arms and pulls them back. Dorothy Comstock sidles up to her, sticks her face in hers. 'So what happened, kiddo?'

'What d'you mean?'

'Don't screw around with us, Cockroft. You've just come out of a meeting. What happened?'

'Nothing.'

Comstock drives a fist into Penny's stomach. It's like being hit by a train. Penny writhes, gasping, fighting to breathe. She needs to double up but Myers pulls up and back, holding her erect.

'I'll ask you again, kiddo,' grates Comstock. 'What happened?'

'I . . . can't breathe. Gonna throw up.'

'Don't gimme a flaming *medical* report. What happened?' Drawing back her fist.

'It was just . . . some people talking.'

'About?'

'School stuff.'

'School stuff like *this*, you mean?' She produces a crumpled paper, smooths it out, reads: 'Subject: Push dosh and how not to pay. *That's* what you've all been rabbiting about, isn't it?'

'If you know, why . . . ohh!' A cramp clenches the girl's abdomen. Unable to bend she lifts her feet, draws up her knees, hangs on her arms for a second's relief.

'Oi!' Myers protests. 'Stand up – I'm not your flipping *mother*.' Over by the door, Lois laughs. 'Nice one, Cassette. Hit her again, Dot Com.'

'No!' Penny shakes her head. 'Yes, it *was* about that. John Passmore in Year Twelve said we should get together, refuse to pay. He says if everybody does it it'll be all right. It's called Pull.'

'Huh?' Dorothy frowns. '*What's* called Pull? What you on about, kiddo?'

'The organization. It's called Pull, like all pull together, y'know? It starts today.'

'Well fancy *that*.' Lois leaves her post, comes over. 'And you're together, eh? All for one and one for all, like the three flipping musketeers?'

'Yeah.'

'So where are they now you *need* 'em, Cockroft?'

46

'Gone home.'

'Right. And that's where they'll be every time somebody needs 'em, and that's why your so-called organization has no chance.' She grabs a handful of the girl's hair, jerks her head up.

'So you'll cough up next Monday, kiddo, like you did today, and your friends better do the same.' She nods at Dorothy, who grins and swings the fist again. Anne Myers lets go and Penny drops to the floor and lies curled like a comma, heaving and gasping and puking gobs of dinner on the tiles.

TWENTY-FOUR

'Come.' Tuesday morning, ten past nine. Dorothy Comstock opens the Head's door, enters, closes it behind her and turns. 'You wanted to see me, sir.' Her tone says she doesn't care one way or the other. Hezzy gazes at her for some time before responding. Dorothy stands with her weight on one foot and an expression of unutterable boredom on her face, staring past his head at the view through the window. The playing field, its far boundary dimmed by mist. A wagtail bounces across the sodden turf in search of breakfast.

'Tell me, Dorothy.' She is not invited to sit. 'Do you work at all? Outside school I mean.'

'No, sir.'

'You must find yourself – you know – a bit hard-up compared to some of your friends. Most of them seem to have part-time jobs of one sort or another.'

'My dad gives me dosh, sir.'

'Lucky girl. So what do you do at weekends, Dorothy?'

Dorothy shrugs. 'Depends, sir.'

'On what?'

'The weather. What's on telly. We hang around the Mall mostly, me and my mates.'

'Would that be Lazenby Mall?'

'It's the only one we've got, sir.' Teetering on the very brink of insolence.

'Were you there last Saturday?' Sharply.

'Saturday?' Mimes thought by frowning at ceiling, brightens. 'Oh yes, sir. I remember 'cause that's the day they found old . . . Mr Dick's little girl there, sir, in the toilets, and I thought wow, I wonder if she was there when *I* –' She breaks off, smiles. '*I* used them toilets, sir, twice. One of 'em anyway.'

The Head's expression is stony. 'I suppose you didn't *see* Mr Dick's daughter last Saturday, Dorothy?'

'*Me*, sir?' Shakes her head. 'No. Never seen her in my life, let alone Saturday.' Frowns.

'Why're you *asking* me, sir – have I *done* something?'

'I don't know, Dorothy. *Have* you?'

'Not that I know of, sir.'

The Head picks up a ballpoint pen, toys with it, trying to make it balance on its tip. He seems to have forgotten Dorothy. She watches him for a while, then yawns to remind him. 'All right, Dorothy,' he growls, without looking up. 'You may go.' She turns and ambles towards the door, managing to look bored even from behind. As she reaches for the handle he murmurs, 'Dot Com?'

'Sir?' She's turned before it dawns. Stands slack-jawed, blushing.

He shakes his head. 'Never mind, Dorothy. Off you go.'

TWENTY-FIVE

Tuesday lunchtime. At the boy's request, Charles Flit-croft meets Gordon Barraclough on a bench in the park. It's a tad cold, and Charles is not amused. He sits hunched, with the collar of his sheepskin car-coat up and his hands in the pockets.

'This better be important, Fax. I'm not the outdoor type.'

'It's important, and I know you don't like me saying stuff on the phone. I think we've got trouble, Mr Flitcroft.'

'What sort of trouble?'

'Both sorts. Adults and kids.'

'Go on.'

'Somebody called a meeting last night, after school. Working kids. Email had a chat with one of 'em when it broke up. Seems they've formed some sort of organization calling itself Pull, and they'll stop paying the ten per cent.'

Charles sighs. 'How much do you make working for me, Fax?'

'Fiver a day, Mr Flitcroft.'

'Fiver a day. Seven days. That's thirty-five a week, clear. Multiply by six comes to two ten, plus wraps. D'you think I shell out two hundred and ten quid every week so you and the others can sit on your butts chewing the fat and puffing draw?'

'No, Mr Flitcroft.'

'You bet I don't. I pay you to take care of the sort of problem you've dragged me out to tell me about, *without* dragging me out.' He looks sidelong at the boy. 'Of course if you can't *do* that – if you can't handle it – there's a hundred kids out there'd jump at the chance to make the sort of dosh I'm paying you.'

Barraclough shakes his head. 'I can handle it, Mr

Flitcroft, no worries. I thought you should know about it, that's all.'

'I don't *want* to know about it, Fax, that's the whole point. I've enough on my plate. You take care of it, employing the usual methods, and the whole thing'll collapse in a few days. You know how kids are. A few spots of blood and they'll be queuing right round the bikeshed to pay.' He stands up. 'I'm off now, I'm busy.'

'There's something else, Mr Flitcroft.'

'*What* else?' He remains standing. 'And make it snappy, I'm cold.'

'Old Hezzy had Dot Com in, first thing. *Called* her Dot Com as well. I don't know how he knows.'

'Somebody's been running off at the mouth, obviously. What did he want her for?'

'He was asking her about Moby's kid – you know – the one that went missing, Saturday?'

'Yes, I . . .' He breaks off, lowers his voice. 'Are you telling me *she* took the kid?'

'Yeah.'

'Oh for *God's* sake.' He glances up and down the pathway. 'What the heck's she wanna go do something like *that* for? Dope and protection, that's one thing. Abduction of a minor's another. I can't afford to risk being associated with it. You better get rid of her.'

'Get . . . ?' The boy's jaw drops.

'No, no, no, I don't mean *that*.' Flitcroft shakes his head. 'You lot'll get me *life* if I don't watch out. What I mean is, get her out of Push. I don't care how you do it, just get rid of her and make sure she doesn't go blabbing to anyone after. Scare the shit out of her. If the law ever proves a connection between me and you lot I don't want to be facing a kidnap charge. Is that clear?'

'Sure, Mr Flitcroft. I'll see to it.'

'Good. And *don't* use your Push names around teachers. Keep a low profile on school premises or you'll find yourselves *working* for your dosh instead of getting it from me. Wait a couple of minutes before you get up.'

Barraclough watches his froglike boss walk off, then saunters back to school devising painful things to do to Dorothy Comstock.

TWENTY-SIX

Three forty-five. Jill, Penny and Jane turn on to Skopje Way. Jill looks at Penny. 'How's it feel to be the founder of a great movement, Pen?'

Penny pulls a face. 'Feels fine, except when I'm being battered by Email and them.' She touches her stomach, where it's still tender. 'I hope they never find out it was my idea, that's all.'

'You're not paying though?'

'*Course* I'm not. How could I? You don't push other people into doing something dangerous then not do it yourself.'

'What bothers me,' says Jill, 'is they might contact Mr Patel, then he'll know we're not paying and sack us.'

Penny shakes her head. 'I don't think they will, Jillo. Patel's got nothing to do with Pull and they know it. They'll go straight for the members.' She shivers. 'And I know exactly what that'll be like.'

'There were sixty-four kids at that meeting,' points out Jane, 'which means Pull has sixty-four members already. Push has six people in school. They can't get us all.'

'Hmmm.' Penny boots a stone into the verge. 'John Passmore was right, you know. The whole thing depends on us sticking together, and we won't really start to find out till next Monday if that's going to happen.'

'If then,' cautions Jane. 'I mean, if nobody pays next Monday, Flitcroft might decide to send in guys from outside school. Older guys. Depends whether he thinks it's worth his while for the bit he gets out of us.'

'*Bit?*' Penny snorts. 'There's hundreds paying. I bet

he takes a thousand a week out of Cottoncroft Comp, and anyway it isn't just the dosh. He'll be worried what might happen in other places if people see us getting away with it. No.' She shakes her head. 'We shouldn't kid ourselves. What we're doing here is threatening Froggy's whole rotten empire, and that's scary. Seriously scary.'

TWENTY-SEVEN

Back Quebec Street, eight p.m. The Cottoncroft Comp chapter of Push in emergency session. Colin Day eyeballs Gordon Barraclough across the cheerless room. 'This better be a *real* emergency, Fax. I'm missing United versus Juventus on the box.'

Barraclough nods. 'It's real, CD.' He grins. 'United'll get stuffed anyway so you're not missing anything.' He checks the semicircle of chairs. Everybody's here. Dot Com slouches in the middle, chewing gum and looking smug. She thinks her exploit last Saturday makes her hero of the hour. She doesn't know this meeting is about her.

'OK, guys, listen up.' He avoids looking at the girl. 'I had a chat with Froggy Flitcroft. I told him about yesterday's meeting and how they launched this organization, Pull. He's not worried, thinks it'll fall apart when we lean on one or two members.' He smiles. '*A few spots of blood* is the way he put it.'

Dot Com nods. 'He's right, and *I* wanna be the one to spill 'em.'

Barraclough has been hoping to work round to the main business gradually, but the daft cow's gone and presented him with an opening so he takes a deep breath and wades in. 'You won't be the one, Dorothy. I mentioned your chat with old Hezzy and Saturday's business came up and Froggy told me to get rid of you.'

The girl gapes. 'Get rid . . . I don't believe you. He *can't* have. I've been in Push longer than anyone here except you. I can't believe he'd —'

'Doesn't matter what you believe, Dorothy — you're out.'

'*Dot Com*,' she cries. 'My name's Dot Com and I've been here longer —'

'It's *Dorothy*,' the boy growls, 'and you better haul your sorry ass out of this *private* meeting unless you want to be carried out in four buckets.'

'But that's so *unfair*.' She appeals to the others. 'Email . . . Cassette . . . *tell* him.'

Lois Baxter shakes her head. 'It's no use, Dot, Froggy's the boss. If he says you're out, you're out.'

'I *know* stuff. Kick me out and I go straight to the law, tell 'em *everything*. The dosh, Flitcrofts, Patel's papers – *everything*. I'll get you done, the lot of you. *Nobody* screws around with me.'

'Dorothy.' Barraclough's voice is soft but his eyes are hard. '*We* know things too, like last Saturday you abducted a little kid from outside its home. Have you any *idea* how long you could go away for, if somebody told 'em it was you?'

Close to tears, Dorothy shakes her head.

'*Life*, Dorothy. If they want they could put you away for life, and d'you know what they call you in prison when you've messed about with a kid? A *beast*. They call you a beast, and you're put in a special wing with all the other beasts so the inmates can't get at you, but they get you anyway, one way or another.' He shakes his head. 'You wouldn't last a week, kiddo, so if I were you I'd get up and walk away and never say a word to anyone about all that stuff you know.'

Dorothy stands up, crosses the damp floor with her head bowed and every eye on her. She's biting her bottom lip so she won't cry. Malcolm Longstaff follows her across the yard, opens the little door in the big door, stands aside. He doesn't speak. As she crosses the threshold she feels the strength that comes from being a part of something fall away.

TWENTY-EIGHT

Wednesday, quarter to nine. A chill morning of thick mist, wet leaves underfoot. Colin Day finds Gary Waterhouse walking the perimeter of the playing field and falls in beside him.

'Forget something, did you?'

Waterhouse pulls a face. 'Don't think so.'

'Do the words "two pounds twenty" mean anything to you?'

'Two pounds twenty? Nope, except I'd sooner have two pounds twenty in my pocket than in yours.'

'In your pocket now, is it?'

'Yes, why?'

'Get it out. You missed Monday.'

'I *know*, you turkey – it was deliberate. No point shelling out and forming Pull the same day.' He knows CD won't resort to violence when he's by himself.

'*Pull.*' The other boy scoffs. 'You think we give a damn about your piddling little outfit, Gaz? Get real, for pete's sake. We're Push. We practically *run* this town, and if you think a bunch of kids're going to change that, you're crazy.' He looks sidelong at Gary.

'We've got orders to spill blood over this, so do yourself a favour and pay up.'

Waterhouse shakes his head. 'Do *yourself* a favour and sod off, Col.' He aims a vicious kick at a clump of dew-laden grassheads, spattering Day's trouserleg with droplets. The wannabe gangster hates being called Col. 'I'll tell you something I've noticed ever since I've been at this school, and I'm not the only one. There's fifty, sixty Asian kids here and most of 'em have jobs. In fact some of 'em work horrendous hours waiting on or sewing, but *they* don't pay Push dosh. They don't get asked, and I know why. It's because they've got organizations of their own: organizations Push doesn't fancy tangling with. Well –' he locks eyes with Day – '*we*'ve got our own organization now and I don't suppose we can bring down Push, but maybe Pull can make it so it's not worth your while trying to collect our little bits of dosh. Maybe we'll make it just hassly enough so your frog-faced boss'll leave us alone like he does the Asians, and that's all we're after.' He smiles tightly. 'You can tell him that if you like. *Col.*'

TWENTY-NINE

Lauren Pascoe delivers the Sundays for Mitchell's on Lofthouse Road. It's a heavy job because the Sundays are fat, and you have to get out of bed early because people like to browse them over breakfast. But at least there's no school. Mr Mitchell pays Lauren three pounds every Sunday. Thirty pence of this goes to Push, leaving her with two pounds seventy for her efforts. She resents this, and if she was at Cottoncroft Comp she'd probably be a member of Pull, but she's at the Catholic school, St Brigit's, so she's never heard of it. The reason Lauren didn't cough up Monday was because she was off school with a headache. She expects to pay double next week.

Push don't know this. The budding rebellion at the Comp has them twitchy, so that Lauren's absence looks deliberate. 'Dangerous,' says Barraclough when a collector at St Brigit's mentions it. 'Could mean this Pull thing's spreading to other schools. We better nip *that* in the bud, sharpish.' It doesn't occur to him that Pull wasn't even launched last Monday morning, which is why Lois Baxter is waiting for Lauren at ten past six when she takes her customary shortcut through some mostly abandoned allotments.

'Morning, Lauren.' She plants herself in the middle of the pathway, forcing Lauren to stop.

'Oh hi, Email. I . . . sorry I wasn't in school Monday.' She knows there's only one reason Lois would be here. 'I'm paying double next week.'

'Liar.'

'No, it's true. I get migraines.'

Lois snorts. 'I don't get up at half-five to hear about migraines, Pascoe. I want my breakfast, not your medical history. It's this Pull thing, isn't it?'

'Pull thing? What d'you mean?'

'I'm warning you, kid – don't mess with me. We know all about it.'

'Well *I* don't, Email. I haven't done anything. I couldn't help being off Monday. Look –' scrabbles in her pocket – 'I've got the money, you can have it *now* if you want.'

Lois steps forward, slaps the coins out of the girl's hand. Lauren gasps. '*Please*, Email – I've got Mass after this. Let me go.'

'No way.' The big girl shakes her head. 'I've a message for St Brigit's.'

'W-what message?'

'*This*.' Lois drives her fist into Lauren's stomach. 'And *this*.' She draws back her foot and kicks the fallen girl in the face, bursting her nose. Lauren covers up, spluttering. Lois bends over her. 'Show yourself to your mates tomorrow. Say *this* is what happens to kids who think they don't have to pay.'

Lauren's sack of papers lies on the path. Lois snatches it up, lugs it to a mouldering rain-barrel, drops it in the water and walks away. Lauren spits blood, snot and bits of gravel on the path. Her attacker, seen through tears, is a receding blur. In the barrel the sack fills up and starts to sink, trailing a rope of bubbles.

THIRTY

'Just a tick, Maisie, before you go rushing off.' Monday teatime. Kath Malin is chopping lettuce at the sink.

'Mu-um.' Maisie is halfway out the door. 'I'll be late for work.'

'You and your work, don't even get a decent meal inside you before you're –'

'I have a school *dinner*, Mum. You'd have me fat as a pig, two dinners a day.'

'Better *that* than a walking skeleton like those supermodels you try to look like. When I was your age –'

'What did you *want* me for, Mum – I'm late.'

Kath dumps a double handful of chopped leaves in a colander. 'Your trainers, love. Haven't seen them lately.'

'No, Mum, they're in my locker at school.'

'Why on earth are they at *school*, Maisie? You're not allowed to wear trainers at school.'

'No, I know, but I took 'em to show my friends and I keep forgetting to bring them home.'

'Well you be sure and remember tomorrow, please. Your dad and I didn't fork out seventy pounds for trainers so you could chuck 'em in the bottom of a locker and forget about them.'

'OK, Mum, sorry.'

'And tell Vi I'll see her day after tomorrow at Waterstones. Two o'clock.'

'What's going *on*, Miss Malin?' Pauline Gadd frowns as Maisie appears, buttoning her overall. Mrs Gadd is manageress at Posh Spice Pickles. Maisie looks at her, startled. 'Nothing, Mrs Gadd. I'm not late or anything, am I?'

The woman shakes her head, looks irritated. 'It isn't that. Your father phoned Mr Snowden's secretary to say you wouldn't be in at *all* this evening – touch of flu or something. I've had to bring a girl through from packing to take your place, and that's left *them* short. I think you'd better put your coat on and go home, Missy, and in future –'

'But my dad *can't* have phoned, Mrs Gadd. He's still at work, and besides there's nothing wrong with me. I've been at school all day.'

'Well, *somebody* claiming to be your father phoned, and now Iris Leyland's in your seat and you'd be no use in packing so we wouldn't be paying you, so you might as well go home. You can come tomorrow, but if anything like this ever happens again I'll finish you on the spot. Plenty of girls out there waiting for your job.'

'Well . . .' Maisie is close to tears. 'Can I just give a message to my auntie? She's over there.' Auntie Vi has turned in her seat and is gazing across, obviously wondering what's happening.

The manageress nods. 'Very well, but don't take all night over it. My department has a quota to fill.'

'*My* department,' growls Vi when Maisie tells her. 'Love 'emselves to bits, some people.' She frowns. 'Funny though, somebody phoning like that. Wonder who it could have been?'

'I've a fair idea, Auntie Vi.'

'*Have* you, love?' She gives her niece a searching look. 'You're not in some sort of trouble, are you, 'cause if you are –'

'No no, no trouble. Listen, I better go – she's watching us. So Mum'll see you Wednesday and I'll see you tomorrow, OK?'

'Right. Mind how you go, love.'

Cardigan Street is deserted as usual. Maisie creeps down the very middle of the road, peering into shadows and trying to make no noise. She refused Colin Day one eighty-eight today, but she gets home without anything happening, then has to loiter outside till her usual time to avoid awkward questions. She's three pounds seventy-five down, whoever made that call might do it again anytime and get her the sack, and she's expected to produce a pair of Nikes for her mum tomorrow.

And this is only the very, very start of it.

THIRTY-ONE

'Hey, what the heck's *happened*, Lauren? How'd you *get* like that?' Josh Winnifrith goggles at the bruises under his girlfriend's eyes, her colourful nose. It's half-seven Monday and they've met as usual at Sizzlers. Sizzlers is Cottoncroft's most popular burger joint and Josh has a job there evenings, clearing tables and keeping the floor clean. He's a big lad, and has acted as bouncer too when needed.

The girl grimaces. 'I had a run-in with Email yesterday, nearly cost me my job.'

'Run-in?' Josh swishes a damp cloth round her table in case the manager's watching. 'What about?'

Lauren shrugs. 'That's the queer thing – I've no idea. She ambushed me on my round. I thought it was 'cause I hadn't paid last Monday but it was something else. *"It's this Pull thing, isn't it?"*, she says, then flattens me. I didn't even know what she was on about.'

Josh nods grimly. 'I do.' He glances towards the servery. 'Go give your order. I'll talk to you in a minute.'

Lauren orders a baconburger with jumbo fries and a tall Coke. She's just put her tray on the table and sat down when he slides into the next seat. ''s OK – Gibbo's on his break.' Gibbo's the manager. 'Listen.' Quickly he tells her about the meeting a week ago, and about Pull. 'I was on the door. Push showed up. They went off when they saw me but we all knew there was bound to be trouble.' He pulls a face. 'Never expected they'd start with someone from St Brigit's, though. Must've thought you were in on it even though it hadn't started then, which shows how thick they are. Anyway.' He stands up, flicks his cloth over the red plastic tabletop. 'Someone's gonna pay for that face of yours, sweetheart. Barraclough'll do.'

'No, listen.' She drops a hand on his. 'I've got a better idea. What if St Brigit's actually *does* get in on

65

Pull? That'll hurt 'em more than Fax getting done over, won't it?'

The boy shrugs. 'Well yeah, but like . . .' He looks at her. 'If you get involved, there'll be more of the sort of stuff you got from Email yesterday. A *lot* more. Are you sure you want the hassle?'

'I'm sure there's plenty of kids at school'd *love* to stand up to the Push. In fact I'm amazed your lot didn't think of involving other schools right from the start. We've as many kids paying Push dosh as you have.'

'OK then, call a meeting. Tell everybody what's happening. Show 'em your bruises so they know it's not a game.' He grins. 'My mates'll be over the moon when I tell 'em St Brigit's is with us.'

'Magic.' Lauren's smile comes out a bit crooked. 'And don't forget the City Tech. *They've* got working kids as well. Fax and them'll soil their undies when they find they're up against a mass movement.'

THIRTY-TWO

'Flitcroft Staff Services, Mavis speaking. How may I help you?'

'Fax. Is Mr Flitcroft there?'

'Mr Flitcroft is out visiting a client, and you've been told to call this number only in emergencies.'

'This *is* an emergency.'

'Then you'd better tell *me*.'

'Well . . . it's a numbers thing really.'

'Numbers? What're you *talking* about?'

'We think St Brigit's is in on Pull. He's told you about Pull, I suppose?'

'Yes he has, and he also told me he told you to sort it without bothering him. It's what you're paid for.'

'That's part of it, Mrs Flitcroft – we *aren't* paid. Not this week anyway. The others're getting twitchy, and what with us being down to five since he made me dump Dot Com, I don't think we're going to be able to stop this Pull thing if it *is* spreading. We need to bring in a few of the older guys.'

'Now listen, Fax. I don't know whether my husband will go for that at all, and you mustn't even *approach* anybody without his say-so. You *haven't*, have you?'

'Course not, I'm not daft. Do I call in the office or what?'

'Absolutely not. I'll speak to Mr Flitcroft and he'll contact you. In the meantime, do nothing. About getting people involved, I mean.'

'OK, only tell him it's urgent. Five against five hundred can't win except in video games. Bye.'

THIRTY-THREE

'Excuse me, Mrs Gadd?' The manageress is perched on the corner of a bench, drinking coffee from a styrofoam cup. She looks up. 'Miss Malin, bright and early. Not handing in your notice, I hope?'

'No, no, I . . . wanted to explain something.'

The woman nods. 'Found out who made that call, did you?'

'Well, not exactly, but it's to do with that.'

'Go on then.'

Maisie glances round the room, surprised how big it looks with only the two of them in it. 'The thing is, some of us at school – some of the kids with jobs – have decided not to pay Push dosh any more.'

'Oh?' Mrs Gadd arches her brow. 'How's *that* going to work?'

'Well, we've started an organization called Pull. If loads of us refuse to pay, there'll be nothing Push can do. That's the idea, anyway.'

'Hmmm. And what has this to do with yesterday's call, Miss Malin?'

'That's what I wanted to explain. You see, Push know I'm in Pull, and I think it was one of them who phoned. You know – to get me in trouble. And I realize they can do it whenever they like and I wanted to say if it happens again can you ignore it please, because it won't be true?'

Mrs Gadd gazes at the girl, shakes her head. 'I don't think I can promise that, Miss Malin. It's all right your saying it won't be true, but how will *I* know? Suppose you're genuinely ill some evening and one of your parents phones? I've no way of distinguishing between that and another hoax call. I'd have to make an alternative arrangement as I did yesterday, just in case. Mr Snowden's running a business here – he needs staff he can rely on.'

Maisie swallows. 'So what do I *do*, Mrs Gadd? I mean I don't want to lose this job, but it won't be *my* fault if somebody rings and tells a lie about me, will it?'

'Well of *course* it'll be your fault, you silly girl.'

'How?'

'Because it's you who've decided not to pay Push, and that's why somebody's trying to get you the sack.'

'But . . . surely you don't think it's *fair*, Mrs Gadd, kids having to pay?'

'Fair?' The woman laughs briefly. 'It's no use talking about what's *fair*, Miss Malin. We have to deal with things as they *are*, and in Cottoncroft working kids pay Push. It may not be fair but it's the way things are, and nobody's going to risk disrupting his business by employing a troublemaker.'

'A . . . troublemaker?' Maisie looks stunned. 'But surely it's the Push who're the troublemakers.'

The woman shakes her head. 'Not as far as employers are concerned, Miss Malin. An employer takes on a young worker and pays her a wage, ten per cent of which goes to Push. The boss gets the job done, the kid's got dosh in her pocket, Push is happy and there's no trouble.' She smiles, shakes her head. 'Take my advice, dear. Pay up. That way the mischievous phone calls will stop, you'll keep your job and you won't let your Auntie Vi down.'

'My auntie?'

'Certainly, Miss Malin, your auntie's involved. She told Mr Snowden what a steady, reliable girl you are. You wouldn't want Mr Snowden to think that was a lie, would you?'

'N-no.'

'Well, there you are.' She glances at the clock. 'The others will start arriving in a minute. You go change into your overall, and think about what I've said. Ninety per cent of a wage is a darn sight better than no wage at all and an unemployed auntie in the family. Off you go, Miss Malin.'

THIRTY-FOUR

As Maisie Malin leaves Posh Spice Pickles at the end of her shift and makes her way disconsolately along Cardigan Street, a taxi draws up in front of Cottoncroft's best hotel, The Adelphi, and a man gets out. There's nothing striking about his appearance. He's a middle-aged man of medium height, wearing a business suit and carrying a scuffed blue suitcase. He has steel-rimmed spectacles, a cropped salt-and-pepper moustache and a polished bald patch, and his shoe heels are a bit worn. He might be a salesman, travelling for a small company.

He might be, but he's not.

The taxi pulls away. The man lugs his case through the revolving door and approaches the desk. The smile of the young receptionist combines a welcome with a question. 'Green,' says the man, though this is not his name. 'Just the one night.'

'Mr Green.' The girl consults a screen. 'Ah yes, there we are. Single with bath, quiet?'

The man nods. 'That's it.'

She hands over a perforated keycard. 'It's two forty-four, sir. You'll find the lifts over there, behind that weeping fig. Enjoy your stay.'

Having located his room and dumped his suitcase, the man closes and double-locks his door before crossing to the window. There'd be no view to speak of even if it were daylight but that's all right. Mr Green's not looking for a view. Privacy's what matters in his line of work. He draws the thick curtains, making sure they overlap in the middle. He even checks there's nobody in the bathroom before unlocking his case and starting to lay out its contents. He has a call to make later, but he won't use the phone in the room. Hotel phones are routed through a switchboard and you never know who's listening.

Mr Green's motto is you can't be too careful, and he never forgets it. That's why he's locked in a hotel room and not in a cell.

THIRTY-FIVE

So what do I do? *What?* Maisie turns into Balaclava Street. A part of her is thankful to have made it home safely but mostly she feels despair. All the way home, Mrs Gadd's words have echoed in her skull. '*You'll keep your job and you won't let your Auntie Vi down.*' What exactly did she mean? What do her words boil down to?

I know very well what they boil down to. If I stay loyal to Pull, and Push make another call like yesterday's, I get the sack and Auntie Vi gets into bother for bringing a so-called troublemaker into the firm. Very likely she gets the sack as well, which will make me really really popular in the family. And if I don't the kids see me as a traitor and a coward, result, zero popularity at school. Terrific choice, huh?

She reaches number nine, walks up the path.

'Hello, love.' Kath Malin smiles at her daughter. 'How'd it go tonight?' She's brewing tea, stacking biscuits on a plate. Maisie crosses the kitchen shrugging off her jacket, drapes it over the banister in the hallway, comes back.

'It was all right, but I'm sick of smelling like a jar of pickled onions all the time.'

Her mother smiles. 'Could be worse, sweetheart – some people work with sewage. By the way, did you give your Auntie V. my message last night?'

'Yes. She said fine.'

'Thanks, love. Carry these through, would you?' Holding out the biscuit plate.

'Sure. Dad's home, then?'

'Uh-huh. Can't you hear the telly?'

Maisie cocks her head on one side, groans. 'Football.'

Her mother sighs. 'What else? Go on through, I'll bring the tea. Oh, and before I forget, you might just slip up to your room and fetch those trainers down. Your dad mentioned them tonight.'

Shit! Maisie carries the biscuits through to the front room, slides the plate on to the coffee table.

Her father smiles. 'Hi, sweetheart, didn't hear you come in.'

She nods at the screen. 'Not surprised with that racket. Who's playing?' She doesn't give a toss who's playing, but with no trainers in her room she's going to need a friend.

'Man U and Ajax at Old Trafford. One apiece, nine minutes left plus stoppage time.'

'Nine minutes is more than enough for United. Three—one it'll be at the end.'

'Hope you're right, sweetheart.' His attention's back on the screen. Maisie leaves the room, creeps up to her own. Mum won't mention trainers while the match is on unless she's looking for a divorce, and if Maisie's quiet when it's over they might think she's gone to bed.

They might.

THIRTY-SIX

Tuesday, late. Charles hangs his jacket over a chairback, sits down and bends forward to unlace his shoes. Mavis looks down at him thinking, *He* is *like a frog*. She says, 'Fax phoned, says he's got a problem.'

'Not *now* Mavis, for God's sake.' He eases off a shoe, wiggles his toes. 'Get us a coffee, will you? I've had a hell of a day.' He enjoys playing the harassed executive.

'"A numbers thing really", is how he put it.'

Charles levers off the other shoe, straightens up, eyeballs his partner. 'Coffee,' he murmurs, '*now*.' He's got something to tell her but he wants a bit of pampering first. Feels he's earned it, deal like this.

'There you go.' Mavis offers the beaker.

He takes it, sips, sighs. 'Sit down a minute, I've something to tell you.' She pulls up a chair, sits.

'Guy phones around ten. I'm clearing up to come home. Says can we meet, he's a proposition to put to me. I tell him I've had a hard day, can't it wait till tomorrow and by the way, who *are* you? "Mr Green," he says. "I'm Mr Green." *Of?* I ask him, and he chuckles. "I represent a very large company," he says. "*Very* large. Customers worldwide and a product that sells itself. Meet me in half an hour at The Adelphi and I guarantee you won't be sorry." "How'd you get my name?" I start to ask, but he's hung up.' Charles shrugs, sips his coffee. Mavis looks at him.

'So, did you go?'

'Oh yes, I went. Nearly didn't but then I thought, hanging up on me like that, that's arrogance, and arrogance comes with success. Mr Green doesn't give a damn whether I turn up or not, he's got something good to offer and doesn't anticipate any shortage of takers. So I went.'

'And?'

Charles turns the beaker between his palms, looks smug. '*And* we're in the money, Sweetness. Money for old rope. Listen.'

THIRTY-SEVEN

Kath Malin knocks on Maisie's door. 'Maisie?' No response. 'Maisie, are you in bed?'

'Uh-huh.'

'But there's tea and biscuits waiting downstairs, and Dad's waiting as well.'

'Dad?'

'Yes. I *told* you he mentioned your trainers, and I want to see them too. Can I come in?' She doesn't wait for permission but opens the door. Maisie's in bed but her bedside lamp is still on. She sits up, sighs and gazes at her mother.

'OK, Mum, I wasn't going to bother you and Dad about this, but I don't have my trainers any more and I'll tell you why.'

Kath sits on the bed and Maisie tells everything, starting the Monday when Gordon Barraclough and Malcolm Longstaff threatened her. Her story is punctuated by interjections from Kath, some incredulous, some indignant. When she's heard the story up to date, Kath goes to the top of the stairs to call her husband and Maisie has to run through the whole thing again.

'It's . . . unacceptable,' splutters Don Malin, pacing the room. 'The whole thing's totally and utterly unacceptable. Bits of kids, hiding behind names like Fax and Walkman, behaving like . . . like James Cagney, Edward G. Robinson, George Raft. And the teachers *let* 'em, that's what gets me. When *I* was at school –'

'It's not the *teachers*' fault, Dad,' protests Maisie. 'Push never do anything openly, they're little angels where teachers can see 'em. It's those Flitcrofts to blame. They're nothing but a pair of crooks, the police ought to chuck 'em in jail.'

'I know, sweetheart, and I'm sure that's exactly what'll happen one of these days.' He looks at her. 'But while they remain at large they're dangerous people and I don't want my daughter getting on the wrong side of them, which is what you've done by joining this Pull campaign.'

'What're you *saying*, Dad – that I should pay up and let all my mates down, is *that* it?'

77

'No, Maisie, what I'm saying is you don't go any-where near Posh Spice Pickles ever again, nor do you take any other paid work till you've completed your education. That way, neither the Flitcrofts nor Push can possibly have any further interest in you, which means you'll be relatively safe, which is what your mother and I want you to be.'

'But Dad . . . what about *dosh*? I'll be skint, the only kid in my class who can't *go* anywhere, join *in* anything. *And* everybody'll think I quit 'cause I'm scared. I'll have no friends, won't dare show my face. I'll have to *kill* myself.'

'Now don't be silly, darling.' Kath reaches for her but Maisie sways out of reach. 'Your dad and I will see you have pocket money, and everybody will know *we* took you out of the pickle factory because you were attacked and robbed on the way home. Mr Snowden can't possibly blame Auntie Vi for your parents taking you away, and your dad's right – if you're not working, you're out of the firing line.'

'Yes, and all my friends'll be *in* the firing line. I wish I hadn't told you. I wish you'd never got me those rotten trainers 'cause they're all you really care about, aren't they? Well, *aren't* they?'

'That's unforgivable, Maisie.'

'So don't forgive me, nobody else will. And now, if you've both finished ruining my life will you please leave so I can cry all night?'

THIRTY-EIGHT

'Got a minute, Lois?' Wednesday, eight-twenty. Josh Winnifrith is leaning on a gatepost as the girl enters the yard. She stops. 'What?'

'Lauren Pascoe.'

'Who's she when she's at home?'

'Oh you know her, Lois. Sunday you gave her papers a bath when you *should've* been getting ready for church.'

'Church?' Lois snorts. 'I don't have time for church, I'm too busy counselling kids who think rules don't apply to them.'

'Is *that* what you call it – counselling?'

'Yeah.'

'Well, let me counsel *you* for a minute, Lois. First off, Lauren's my girlfriend, and *nobody* messes with my girlfriend. If they try, *this* happens.' He darts forward, grabs the girl's wrist and squeezes, gazing into her eyes as he gradually tightens his grip. Lois snarls and spits, raining blows with her free fist on her assailant's head, chest and shoulders. Josh ducks and sways to keep his face clear of slashing nails, all the time tightening his grip. Kids are stopping to watch, so he moves the show clear of the gateway in case a teacher's car appears. Lois kicks and writhes but has no choice than to follow her tormentor. There are tears in her eyes, she can't keep them back, and she knows the growing clot of spectators is enjoying her plight.

'Gerroff, Winnifrith,' she snarls, 'or you'll be sorry when we get you by yourself.' His response is to squeeze even harder, so hard she's shocked a human hand can deliver such pressure. The pain is so intense she loses control and starts to howl, hopping from foot to foot to the amusement of the watchers. Winnifrith's face remains impassive as he tightens his grip to its limit and holds it there.

Lois Baxter stops hopping. Her legs buckle and she collapses on to the tarmac where she kneels weeping till he lets her go.

'And second,' he hisses, bending over her as she folds forward to cradle her throbbing wrist, 'St Brigit's is in on Pull, and that's *your* fault for picking on Lauren. I don't think your dumb mates'll be too chuffed about that, and I *know* Froggy Flitcroft's going to hate it.' He chuckles. 'And that's the end of your counselling session, but there's plenty more if I hear you're in need of it.' He straightens up, glowers round at the spectators. 'OK you lot, show's over, bog off.'

Nobody shouts for an encore.

THIRTY-NINE

'Now.' Miss Day beams at her class. She's been teaching less than a month, it's the start of a new day and she's chockful of enthusiasm. 'Which Christian festival did we decide is most like Diwali? Yes, Sarah-Jane?'

'Christmas, miss.'

'Correct. And in what ways are the two festivals similar?'

'Miss, Diwali's the festival of lights – they have lamps and that – and Christmas there's like candles and those little lights you hang on the tree.'

'Symbolizing the light of the world, that's right, Sarah-Jane.' She smiles. 'It's good to know *somebody* was sitting up and taking notice last week.'

'Sarah-Jane Allinson, creep creep creep.'

'*What* did you say, Joshua Winnifrith?'

'Nothing, miss. And it's Josh.'

'It didn't *sound* like nothing, and you're Joshua in my class because that's the name your parents chose for you.'

Josh grimaces. 'Tell me about it. Damn near ruined my life. D'you know what we call *you*, miss?'

The teacher sighs. 'No, but I suspect you're about to tell me.'

'Judgement.'

She frowns. 'Judgement?' The class titters. 'Why Judgement, Joshua?'

'Judgement *Day*, miss. RE teacher, *Judgement Day*, geddit?'

'Oh – oh *right*.' Miss Day chuckles. 'Spot on. Whose flash of inspiration was that?'

'Dunno, miss. They just like *happen*, teachers' nicknames.'

'Yes well, I have to admit mine's clever, but this *is* an RE class in your GCSE year so we'd better press on. On the board are ten questions on the subject of Hinduism.' She turns the board on its swivel so they can see the questions. 'You are to write down your answers in . . . what's the *matter*, Lois?'

'Can't write, miss.'

'Whyever not, Lois?'

'Miss, Joshua crushed my wrist. It kills.'

'Joshua . . . ?' She shoots the boy a look, goes over to Lois's table. 'Show me.'

Lois extends her arm. The wrist is bruised and puffy, dark against the white of the shirtcuff. The teacher swallows, she expected something trivial. 'You say *Joshua* did this?'

'Yes, miss, in the yard before school.'

'Joshua?' She looks a horrified question at the boy. He shrugs.

'She had it coming, miss.'

'What on earth do you *mean*, she had it coming?' She shouts this, startling the class because she never raises her voice. 'You're a *boy* for heaven's sake, and a big one at that. You can't go grabbing a girl . . . grabbing her, inflicting damage of this sort, no matter what she's – it's . . . it's *assault*. I think you'd better come with me, Joshua Winnifrith. You too, Lois. This is a matter for the Head.'

FORTY

'Come.' Pauline Day opens the Head's door, shepherds the pair into the presence. Hezzy looks surprised. 'Miss Day – what's this?'

'I'm sorry, Mr Tate, but I thought I'd better be guided by you on this one. Show the Head your wrist, Lois.'

'Oh, mi-iss.' Lois doesn't want this. She'd have kept her injury to herself if she'd known Hezzy was going to be involved. Reluctantly she extends her hand over his desk, pulls up the cuff. Tate inspects the swollen wrist, looks quizzically at the teacher.

'As you see, Mr Tate, it's badly bruised and the thing is, Lois says Joshua did it and he doesn't deny it. In fact he says she had it coming.'

'Does he now?' Hezzy gestures to Lois to take her hand away, gazes up at Winnifrith. Like Dorothy Comstock before him, Josh is staring out of the window to show how bored he is.

'Joshua?'

'Sir?' He starts, as though finally noticing the Head's presence.

'*Are* you responsible for the state of this girl's wrist?'

'No, sir. I did it, but *she's* responsible. She beat my girlfriend up.'

'I didn't, sir.'

'Yes you did, you *know* you did.'

'Sir, it all happened outside school hours so it's private, between me and him.'

'So why did you go blabbing to the teacher, you –'

'Shut up, the pair of you!' Hezzy leaps to his feet. 'How *dare* you engage in a slanging match in my study? You.' He jabs a finger at Josh. 'You ought to be ashamed of yourself. A great hulking lad like you, using your physical strength to injure someone half your size. And *you*.' He glares at Lois. 'I'll have you to understand that *nothing's* private between students of Cottoncroft Comprehensive. While you are pupils here your conduct is *my* business, wherever or whenever it takes place. Is that clear?'

'Sir.'

'Is it clear to *you*, laddie?'

'Sir.'

'I should think so.' He sinks into the swivel chair and sits gazing at the two of them. They're staring at the window again, but the show of indifference is looking decidedly strained. After a moment he says, 'You, Joshua, can thank your lucky stars the police aren't involved in this matter. I have no doubt that if they were, you'd be looking at a trip to court on a serious charge. Actual Bodily Harm, perhaps. Might even be sent away. And make no mistake, if that happened you'd find yourself among lads far harder than yourself, muscular though you are. And the same might happen to you, Lois, if it's true you beat up some girl. How d'you think your parents would feel if they knew their son, their daughter, was behaving like some sort of gangster? Would they feel proud? *Would* they?'

'No, sir.'

'No, sir.'

'Well, I can promise you this. If either of you is brought before me again for any misconduct involving violence or the threat of violence, I shall not hesitate to involve both your parents *and* the police. I will not have students behaving like hooligans, disrupting the work of my school as you two have disrupted it this morning, bringing shame on the name of

Cottoncroft Comprehensive.' He gazes at them in turn. 'You will both apologize, in writing, to Miss Day for the trouble you have caused her, and from now on I expect to hear only good things about the pair of you. Off you go.' He nods at the teacher. 'You were right to bring the matter to my attention, Miss Day. Thank you.'

FORTY-ONE

Ten-fifteen. A cold, blustery evening with drizzle in the wind. Charles Flitcroft parks the BMW on Manchester Road and strides into Back Quebec Street. He walks with his head down, partly because of the rain but mostly because he's anxious not to be seen in this bit of Cottoncroft at night. If push ever comes to shove, no play on words intended, the last thing he'll need is a witness popping up to say he saw the defendant in Back Quebec Street on such-and-such a date.

'Who is it?' Colin Day's on door duty.

'Flitcroft,' raps Charles, glancing nervously up and down the street. CD opens up.

'Hi, Mr Flitcroft, didn't expect to see —'

'Shut it.' Colin's not sure whether Froggy means

the door or his mouth so he closes both. The man pauses while his eyes adjust to the gloom. 'Where's Barraclough? I'm sick of this.'

'He's inside, Mr Flitcroft.'

'Where we'll *all* be if somebody doesn't get a grip pretty soon. Don't open that door to *anyone*, understand?'

'Never do, Mr Flitcroft.'

'What's going *on*, Barraclough?' The boy shoots out of his easy chair at the sound of his boss's voice. 'There's nothing coming in from schools. Nothing.'

'N-no that's right, Mr Flitcroft. The City Tech's joined Pull, or rather half of it has. I told your wife on the blower, it's spreading. We can't cope.'

The man nods impatiently. 'She mentioned it, that's why I'm here. What d'you want?'

'More guys, basically.'

'Like who, *basically*?'

'Well, I thought Biff, for one.'

'Your *brother*?' Flitcroft frowns. 'You surely don't need a grown man to sort out a handful of –'

'More than a handful, Mr Flitcroft, and you've told me yourself Biff's the best. He'll want dosh of course, but with him and Sparky Sparks on the job we'll smash Pull in a week or two. It'd be worth it.'

'Hmmm.' Flitcroft stands a moment, thinking, *Mr Green. Dosh there, no danger. Pots and pots of it, but not with Pull in the picture. Scare him off that could, and I'm not letting a bunch of silly kids ruin the biggest deal I've ever landed.*

'Yes, OK.' He nods. 'You'll have Biff and Sparky but *listen –*' his eyes lock on to Barraclough's – 'once you've got 'em, I expect you to wipe out this pathetic protest quick-sticks. I've an important deal in the pipeline, and I wouldn't be in your shoes if you let it get loused up, so get a grip.' His gaze takes in the twitchy group. '*All* of you.'

FORTY-TWO

'Are you flipping *lost*, Winnifrith?'

Josh stops. He has no choice, the two men who've stepped out in front of him block Laycock's Ginnel completely. 'How d'you mean, lost? I'm due at Sizzlers.' He sounds cool but his heart thumps his ribs like it wants to get out. He recognizes one of these men. Biff Barraclough, Gordon's big brother. Jailbird, junkie, a deputy boss of Push – the perfect guy not to meet in a dark alley at night.

'No,' says the other guy, 'you're *not* due at Sizzlers, you don't work there any more. You're going home, only you seem to have lost your way.'

'Yeah,' nods Biff, 'so we're like *redirecting* you 'cause

that's the sort of guys we are. I'n't that right, Sparky?'

'Oh, yeah,' Sparky nods, 'helpfulness is my mate's middle name, and gentleness is mine, *except* when someone messes us about.'

'Hoooh!' Rueful shake of the head from Biff. 'Different story then. We've been known to resort to *violence* when someone messes us about, 'specially Sparky here. Seen 'im lose all control, I have. Not a pretty sight.'

Sparky nods. 'Yeah, I'm on tablets for it. So, it's back to the end, turn right, keep going till you see the Poundstretcher sign on your right, turn left and first left again and it's straight in front of you. You can't miss it.'

Josh shakes his head. 'I'm not off back, I'll be late for work.' He knows what will happen, is appalled that seasoned toughs like these are involved, but what choice is there? If the Schwarzenegger of Year Eleven caves in, so will every kid in the school. Biff treats him to a cold stare.

'You're not dealing with little girlies now, Winnifrith. *We* won't dance and wet our knickers if you squeeze our wrists, it'll be the other way round. Go home lad, watch *Time Team*.'

'No.'

He doesn't even see the blow that fells him. There's a flash of blinding pain and he collapses, squashing his nose on the tarmac. Boots come swinging from all directions, thudding into his ribs, his stomach, his spine. So heavy are the blows that his body jumps, flops, jumps again as the two men take turns kicking him. Instinctively he curls up, wrapping his arms round his head. There's gravel in the blood in his mouth. Pain is everywhere. There are voices, lights, a face that gets smaller, going away . . .

FORTY-THREE

'Civilized behaviour.' Hezzy gazes down on the rows of assembled pupils. It is Monday morning and School Meetings are on Friday afternoons. The faces looking up at him are puzzled. He lets his pause lengthen in the hope that this might lend weight to the gravity of his theme. The youngsters shuffle, frown, glance sidelong at one another. The teachers seated behind him on the dais stare at their knees, looking grave.

'We stand poised,' the Head continues, 'on the frontier between two centuries. The twentieth, in which mankind has demonstrated his genius for tech-nological advance while managing at the same time to plumb new depths of cruelty and destruction, and the twenty-first, in which it is to be hoped our moral advancement might begin to match our technological progress so that, instead of finding new and more efficient ways of killing our sisters and brothers, we might seek to help them by alleviating the evils of sickness, poverty and ignorance. In short, it is to be hoped that we might commence to demonstrate civilized *behaviour*, instead of calling ourselves civilized while behaving like barbarians, which is what we've done up to now.' He pauses for effect and goes on. 'Notice my use of the words "*it is to be hoped*", for I chose them carefully. It is to be *hoped* that the new century will see the rise of a wiser, gentler humankind, though it grieves me to have to say that I detect no trace up to now of its emergence. On the contrary, it seems to me that our allegedly intelligent species, or at least that cross-section of it represented by the pupils of Cottoncroft Comprehensive School, is intent on plumbing the abyss of barbarism. On Saturday evening, Joshua Winnifrith of Year Eleven was set upon and savagely beaten in the town centre, and information in my possession seems to suggest that his attackers may be here, in this hall, even as I speak.'

He pauses, letting his gaze pass over the heads of Years Nine and Ten to settle on the seniors towards the rear. 'If this is true – if Winnifrith's assailants *are* present – let me assure them that I will not rest till they are identified, and that when they are I shall not hesitate to involve the police. Joshua Winnifrith is lying in the Infirmary with serious injuries, and those responsible face grave charges. It goes without saying that they also face immediate expulsion from this school. It is my intention that a small but significant segment of that wiser, gentler humankind I spoke of a minute ago shall emerge from Cottoncroft Comprehensive, and woe betide *any* pupil whose mindless thuggery obstructs that intention.'

He remains for a moment, relaxed, fingers curled round the edges of the lectern, gazing down, then adds, 'If anybody should wish to talk to me, about anything at all, I shall be in my study for the rest of the day.' He turns, nods to the teachers and leaves the dais. The swell of young voices seems to lift the teachers for they rise together and are swept into the rips and currents of a new, turbulent week.

FORTY-FOUR

'You said if anybody wanted to –'

'Yes, Dorothy, I did.' Elbows on desktop he steeples his fingers, props his chin on them and looks into the girl's eyes. 'Well?'

Dorothy shuffles her feet, looks at the carpet. 'The boys, sir . . . them you mentioned. I know who they are.'

The Head nods. 'I wondered if you might, Dorothy. Or is it Dot Com?'

'No it's not, sir. Not now. It was Gordon Barraclough and Malcolm Longstaff, and Colin Day might have been there too, sir.'

'How do you know it was them, Dorothy?'

''Cause they're in Push, sir, and Josh Winnifrith got on the wrong side of 'em.'

'Oh – how, exactly?'

'Well, for a start he's in Pull, and then he hurt Lois Baxter.'

'Yes, I know about the Lois Baxter incident, but I don't see how that connects with the so-called Push.'

'She's one of 'em as well, sir. Email, they call her. Email the female.'

'*Lois* is a member of this gang, as well as yourself?'

'I'm not, sir. They booted me out.'

'Ah, and *that's* why you're telling me all this. I thought for a minute your conscience was pricking you, Dorothy.'

'Born without one, sir.'

Hezzy's smile is sardonic. 'I'm sure. You said Winnifrith was in Pull. What's Pull?'

'Some of the kids've decided they won't pay Push dosh any more, sir. They've started a group called Pull.'

'Ah, I *see*, and of course the Push can't let 'em get away with it or our friends the Flitcrofts will be displeased. *That's* why there's been an upsurge of thuggery these last few days. Tell me, Dorothy, why did the Push kick you out?'

'I . . . dunno sir, they just did.'

'Oh *come* now, Dorothy. Even thugs have reasons for what they do. Why would they turn on one of their own just when they've got their hands full with these non-payers?'

'Like I said, sir, I dunno.'

He regards her narrowly. 'Could it be because you did something by *yourself*, Dorothy?'

'Such as what, sir?'

'Oh.' He shrugs. 'Something that frightened them perhaps, because it was a bit extreme. Something you did to work off a personal grudge.'

'*What* grudge, sir? I've no grudge against anyone.'

'No? Nobody been calling you names? Muppet, for example?'

'Well OK, I get Muppet sometimes but it doesn't bother me. I mean, I wouldn't – ' she breaks off, frowning – 'I came trying to help, sir, and now you're treating me like a . . . a . . .'

'Kidnapper?'

'No!' Vehement shake of the head. 'I wasn't going to say that, I was going to say like a criminal. I've told you everything, there's nothing else so can I go now, sir?'

He gazes at her thinking, *By Jove, I believe Dick's*

right, she did it. Dorothy Comstock abducted his child. He sighs. 'Yes, Dorothy, you're free to go. For now, anyway. Thank you for the information.'

At the door she hesitates, turns. 'Sir, you wouldn't . . . ?'

'Reveal my sources?' He shakes his head. 'Least of your worries, Dorothy. Oh, and Dorothy?'

'Sir?'

'Don't grieve for the Push, you're better outside than in.'

'Yes, sir, thank you, sir.'

FORTY-FIVE

Pull! Pull! Pull!
Meeting 3.30 Monday Year 12 common room
Subject: How are we doing?
All Pull members welcome.

This time there's no need to guard the door. With Hezzy on the warpath, Messrs Barraclough, Longstaff, Myers, Baxter and Day are among the first to vacate the premises when the buzzer brings lessons to a close. The Cottoncroft chapter of Push is keeping a low profile.

John Passmore does a swift count and is gratified. Last time there were sixty-four present, now he makes it eighty-one, and that's not counting Josh Winnifrith.

'Right, can we have a bit of hush, please?' The hubbub fades. Expectant faces gaze at the big Year Twelve, who seems to have become the campaign's unofficial co-ordinator. He glances at the A4 sheet in his hand, clears his throat. 'Thanks for giving up your free time to stay after school again. I know some of you have jobs to go to tonight, and we've all got homework so I won't go banging on.

'Basically what I want to say is, we're doing very well.' A ragged cheer. 'There are eighty-two of us now as against sixty-four a fortnight ago, and that's only Cottoncroft. I was down the City Tech this lunchtime, and they estimate they've got about seventeen members so far.'

'*Seventeen*,' hoots someone at the back, 'to our eighty-two?'

'Ah yes,' confirms Passmore, 'but you've got to remember there's only two hundred kids in the whole place, compared to over a thousand here. I think they're doing brilliantly, considering. And Lauren Pascoe down St Brigit's says forty have joined there, so altogether Pull has a hundred and thirty-nine members.'

Another cheer, and somebody yells, 'Up the rebels!'

Passmore nods, smiles. 'Yes, the score's definitely

96

Pull one, Push nil, but the game's only just kicked off, and there *is* a downside.' He waits for some good-natured booing to subside. 'We've taken three casualties. Josh Winnifrith you know about. He's the worst. Some of you may have heard what happened to Lauren Pascoe a couple of Sundays ago. If not, she was ambushed on her paper-round, beaten up and had all her papers dumped in a rain barrel. Her boss, Mr Mitchell, says if it happens again he'll have to sack her, but she's not paying *and* it was her got Pull started at St Brigit's.'

A long, loud cheer this time. Passmore lets it run its course, then nods. 'Brave kid. When it's *your* turn, think about young Lauren. Might help.' He pulls a face. 'Fact is though, that however we see ourselves, in our parents' eyes we're just kids, and because of that we don't have total control of our actions. I'm mentioning this because our third casualty, who was actually our first, has been pulled out of work by her folks. She's not here, thinks she's let us down, but that's not true. She was beaten up and had her new trainers pinched, and because it happened when she was on her way home from Posh Spice Pickles her parents won't let her out at night. Can't blame them, and certainly can't blame *her*. It's Maisie Malin, and I don't want to hear of anyone slagging her off over this. Remember, it could happen to any one of us – even me.' He shrugs. 'I think that's all, unless anybody has anything to add.' His eyes scan the audience. No hand goes up, and he's about to declare the meeting closed when there's a knock on the door. 'Come.'

His mimicry of the Head's customary invitation causes laughter in the room, but this fades rapidly when the door opens and the man himself stalks in.

FORTY-SIX

'May I?' The youngsters watch silently as a blushing John Passmore yields the floor. For half a minute the Head surveys the packed common room without speaking. They assume he's getting his mad up but he isn't. He's counting.

'Eighty-one.' His face gives nothing away. The eighty-one shuffle and avoid his gaze. 'Eighty-one members of an organization known as Pull, is that correct?'

Nods here and there, mumbles of, 'Sir.'

The Head nods. 'I saw the notice, thought I'd pop in.' His eyes move from face to wary face. The tension mounts. He clears his throat. 'Organizations such as yours, dedicated to the overthrow of established order, have no place in school.' His words draw a sibilant sound from his audience; a collective exhalation. Now they know exactly where he's coming from; where he stands. 'This campaign of yours has precipitated a string of violent incidents in which pupils of my school have been injured, and as Head my duty is clear.'

'Oh but, *sir . . .*' The voice tails off as the Head turns to look at its owner. He recognizes Penelope Cockroft of Year Nine.

'Yes, Penelope?'

The girl's cheeks flare. Her outburst was involuntary, she has no idea how to follow it up.

'Sir, what about the Push? I mean . . . like . . .'

'Excuse me, sir.' John Passmore is on his feet. 'I think what Penelope means is, we've got kids in Push and that's an organization. Why is it that this is tolerated, whereas *our* group –'

'Thank you, John, I was coming to that.' He doesn't say '*before I was so rudely interrupted*', but the implication is there.

Passmore resumes his seat with a muted, 'Sorry, sir,' and smiles briefly to acknowledge a grateful look from Penny. The Head continues.

'My duty is clear, or would be in normal circumstances. Where circumstances are *other* than normal a degree of . . . ah . . . *flexibility* may be in order, and I believe the situation in which you people find yourselves – a situation in which you are being exploited and intimidated by out-and-out racketeers – constitutes an *abnormal* circumstance. Therefore I propose to be flexible to the degree that, far from demanding the disbandment of Pull, I will commend its courage and urge that its efforts be redoubled, until . . .'

He is forced to break off, his voice swamped by the roar which bursts from eighty throats. John Passmore jumps to his feet facing them. 'Listen . . . please, the Head hasn't fin – oh, what the heck – COME ON THEN – THREE CHEERS FOR OLD HEZZY. HIP-HIP . . .'

They are rousing cheers; so rousing the Head feels disposed this once to overlook the Hezzy bit, and even the old. Having got the business of acclamation off its collective chest the audience settles down and the Head continues. '. . . Until the gangsters in our midst – and you *all* know who I mean – are obliged to *work* for a living instead of battening on the powerless, or should I say on those who were *once* powerless, but who are powerless no longer.'

If there's more it'll have to keep for another occasion. In a scrape and clatter of chairs the meeting adjourns itself and the ruffled Head finds himself borne aloft on the dangerously swaying shoulders of ecstatic pupils.

FORTY-SEVEN

Five twenty-five. At Fabrications Inc., the evening shift is clocking on. Sandy swerves her bike between stragglers, props it against the factory wall and glances at her watch. No time to fit the lock but it'll probably be OK here in the yard. She hurries towards the doorway. Big Marge is on the step as usual, scowling at latecomers. She's the overlooker. Behind her loiters Beryl, waiting for her friend.

'Made it then, Sand?'

'Nick of time, Bez. Talk about rush.'

'Oh but it was worth it, right?' Beryl's eyes shine. 'Wasn't he *magic*, old Hezzy? Who'd have thought it?'

'*I* thought he'd come to play hell, mess everything up.'

'*Everybody* did, 'specially when he said that about his duty. I thought, *oh-oh, here comes the chop*, then suddenly –' she laughs – 'it was the best moment of my life, Sand, and that *includes* when Oasis came to open Next in Lazenby Mall.'

'Aw, come *on*,' Sandy protests. 'It was good, but that's right over the top.' She's serious suddenly.

'Truth *is*, Bez, a bit of me hoped it *was* the end of the line. Quite a big bit.'

'Hmmm.' Beryl nods. 'I know what you mean. If they can put old Schwarzenegger in hospital, what might they do to us weaklings? I still feel a whole lot better though, knowing Hezzy's on our side. Hey –' she grins – 'maybe he'll *expel* Barraclough and Long-staff and –'

'I'll expel the pair of *you* if you're not grafting in five seconds flat.' Big Marge has closed the door and is bearing down on them. 'Mr Gossage doesn't pay good wages so you two can stand gossiping all night.'

'Mr Gossage doesn't pay good wages, *period*,' mutters Beryl. Sandy giggles. They hurry to their places.

FORTY-EIGHT

'Hello, Josh,' murmurs Penny. She knows by the slow way he turns his bandaged head that it hurts him to move. He looks at the three girls and says 'Hi' and it's obvious he's wondering why they're here. Penny smiles.

'I'm Penny, this is Jill and she's Jane. We're in Year Nine.'

He tries to nod, winces. 'I know and I don't want

to sound like, *rude* or anything, but why're you visiting me? I mean, you don't really *know* me, right?'

Penny shrugs. 'We're in Pull same as you and that's why we came, 'cause Pull was our idea.' She pulls a face. 'It's our fault, what happened to you. If we hadn't –'

'Naw!' Josh shakes his head, groans and says through clenched teeth, 'There's no way it's your fault, so forget it. It's *time* somebody stood up to those Flitcrofts.' He chuckles painfully. 'Trouble is, we've been so successful they've called up the big fellas to help 'em out.'

Jane frowns. 'Big fellas . . . *what* big fellas?'

'Biff Barraclough, guy called Sparky. Adult Push, and we all know *what* they push.'

'And that's who . . . ?' She turned to the other two. 'I *told* you – I *said* Barraclough and his mates could never have . . . *didn't* I, Penny?'

Penny nods distractedly, staring at Josh. 'So it's *men* fighting us now?'

'Looks like it, yeah.' He attempts a reassuring smile. 'I don't think they'd do anything to girls though – especially girls your age. It's Cassette and Email you've got to look out for.'

'Oh, I dunno about that.' Penny shakes her head. 'I reckon Froggy Flitcroft'll do *anything* to beat Pull, including setting grown-ups on girls. I wonder if we can get any grown-ups on *our* side?'

'We've *got* one,' grins Jill, 'Old Hezzy.'

The injured boy frowns. 'Hezzy?' Briefly, Jill tells him about that afternoon's meeting and the Head's interruption of it. When she's finished, Josh chuckles delightedly. 'That's magic, I feel better already.' He winks. 'I've got some good news as well.'

'What?'

'A reporter was here from the *Target*. This afternoon. Wanted to know all about what he called my *ordeal*. I told him about Biff and Sparky and he called it disgusting, a shame on Cottoncroft. I think he's gonna print something about the Flitcrofts. Something bad.'

'Oooh, I *hope* so!' Penny's eyes shine. 'The Push'll be reeling. Think of it: first old Hezzy declares war on 'em, then the *Target*. I think we're going to *win*, I really do.'

Josh arches his brow, one of the few things he can do without pain. 'I hope you're right, Penny, but all the same I think you better be especially careful these next few days. It'll be great if the *Target does* come out against Froggy and the Push but it'll turn 'em nasty before it brings 'em down, and I want to see the three of you here next week, safe and sound.' He grins. 'I don't get many visitors.'

FORTY-NINE

'You thick, ignorant grommits.' Spit flies from Charles
Flitcroft's mouth as he paces the dank floor, laying
into Biff and Sparky. 'I said put the frighteners on
'im, not half kill him so he ends up in traction with
half the world's press sniffing round. You're dealing
with *kids*, for pete's sake. All you had to do was let
the lad see you, show him what he's up against, but
no – you have to give him a good kicking so he'll
look pathetic in the front-page photo. Well, if you
think I'm going to pay you for a cock-up like this
you're sadly mistaken.'

'And you're mistaken if you think you're *not*,'
rumbles Biff from the armchair. '*Look* at me, Froggy.
I'm not fifteen any more. I'm six-foot three and sixteen stone. You can't talk to me like you used to.'
He snorts. 'We *didn't* half kill the kid, Dudley West
from the *Target* isn't exactly the world's press and
we're mercenaries, Sparky and me – we work for
dosh.' He grins like a wolf. 'And the thing about
mercenaries is they can always pack up and go home
or even change sides, so –' he gets to his feet – 'you
hand over the dosh some time in the next seven

seconds or it'll be *your* picture on the front page of the *Target*, only nobody'll know it's you 'cause you'll be unrecognizable.'

Flitcroft gazes at Biff Barraclough, whom he remembers when he was a twitchy runt of a kid with red-rimmed eyes and a runny nose, and reaches for his wallet, marvelling at the changes a few short years can bring. The junior members watch in awe as large coarse banknotes are counted on to Biff's shovel-like palm. They notice how Biff doesn't even glance at the wad, how his cold shark's eyes stay fixed on Froggy Flitcroft's shifty face till the counting stops and the empty wallet goes back in the inside pocket. When they grow up, each one of them wants to be in every way like Biff.

FIFTY

''Scuse me, sir?'

'Yes, what is it?' Andrew Vessels scowls at the youngster in the doorway.

'Mr Tate says can he see Malcolm Longstaff and Gordon Barraclough in his study straight away.'

'Yes, all right.' The biology teacher doesn't like his lessons interrupted, especially when he's teaching a

GCSE class. The messenger hears his irascibility and withdraws. Blood glowers at the two boys. 'You'd better go, but don't take all day over it because there's *always* a question about the lymphatic system and believe me, neither of you can afford to drop marks when the big day comes.'

'Big flipping day,' growls Longstaff as the pair slouch along the corridor. 'We should've told him we don't give a stuff about his rotten exam.'

'Never mind that,' grunts Barraclough, 'start thinking about what Hezzy wants. He won't have sent for us so he can decide which of us to make Head Boy.'

'It'll be about his flamin' lecture yesterday, won't it – *civilized behaviour.* Daft old sod.'

'No, Malc, that's my point exactly – he's *not* daft. We're going to have to watch it in there, not let anything slip out.'

'What's to slip?' Longstaff widens his eyes. 'We're model pupils, aren't we – never a minute's trouble since the day we started.'

'Yeah, well watch it, that's all I'm saying.' They've reached Hezzy's door. Barraclough knocks.

'Come.' The boys mouth the word with perfect synchronicity and giggle, straightening their faces as they go in. Hezzy is sitting behind his desk, hands clasped on a foam rubber mouse mat. He frowns up at them, goes straight for the jugular.

'I'm told the two of you know something about

Saturday's assault on Joshua Winnifrith. Is that so?'

'*Me*, sir?' Barraclough looks astonished. 'I don't know anything about it, didn't even know he'd been hurt till you told us, sir.'

Longstaff shakes his head. 'Same here, sir. Didn't even know.'

The Head sighs. 'I expected you both to deny it, of course, but understand this: the days when pupils at my school were able to give themselves names like Fax and Walkman and indulge in organized thuggery are over. Oh, yes –' he nods as the boys glance at each other – 'I know your names, individual *and* collective. The *Push*.' His lip curls. 'D'you know the origin of that? I don't suppose you do so I'll tell you. It's Australian. Name given to gangs operating in Sydney a long, long time ago. I expect it was Charles Flitcroft's idea to call his collection of pimps and pushers that, eh?'

Barraclough looks perplexed. 'Charles *Flitcroft*, sir?'

'Yes, yes lad, don't insult my intelligence by pretending you've never heard of the man. Look.' He leans forward. 'I'm aware I can't *prove* the two of you beat young Winnifrith, not at the moment, but it will come, that proof, and in the meantime I want you to know that I'm on to you, and I'm not the only one. From today the pair of you are under intense surveillance and so are Day, Myers and Baxter, *a.k.a.* CD, Email and Cassette. Let any one of you so much as *breathe* in the direction of another of my pupils and I'll be down on the lot of you like a ton of bricks.' He sketches a gesture of dismissal. The boys turn and leave. Rain spatters on the window.

FIFTY-ONE

'Has the *Target* come, Mum?' Tuesday teatime.

Catherine Hall nods while continuing to stir the gravy. 'Yes, it's on the table in the hallway. Why?'

'Oh, just something I have to check out.' Jill heads for the hallway, peeling off her blazer.

Her mother says, 'Hang on, love, I've something to tell you.'

'What?'

'It's bad news, I'm afraid. Come and sit down a minute.'

Jill hangs her blazer over the chairback and sits. 'What?'

'I've had a call from Mr Patel.'

'What about? They haven't messed up his papers again, have they?'

'I don't know, darling, he didn't say. Something must have happened though, because he's letting all his delivery girls go.'

'What d'you . . . are you saying I've got the *sack*?'

'I'm afraid so, darling, yes. You and the others.' She looks her daughter in the eye. 'You didn't tell your dad and me you weren't paying the Push, Jill.'

'Well, *course* I didn't, Mum – it's a kid thing, our own organization.'

'Oh, *Jill*.' Her mother shakes her head. 'It's *not* a kid thing defying the Push. They hurt people who go against them – *cripple* them sometimes. Your dad and I don't want –'

'You're saying I should *pay*, Mum? Is that what you and Dad want? You said *yourself* the Flitcrofts're a blight, so some of us got together to fight 'em, that's all.'

'Yes, dear, I understand and it's very brave, but –'

'But not *your* kid, right? Let others take the risks, enjoy the benefit if they win.'

'You're not being *fair*, darling, and anyway you haven't got a job now, so there's nothing *to* pay.'

'No and you're *glad*, aren't you, you and Dad?'

'Your dad will be relieved, darling, as I am. Relieved you're safe, out of it. It's the *law*'s job to see to the Flitcrofts, the Push. Leave it to the law.'

'Oh sure.' Jill scrapes back her chair, stands. 'It's done a great job so far hasn't it – the law?'

She flounces out of the kitchen and up the stairs, snatching the *Target* from the hall table as she passes. Sitting on her bed she riffles through the pages till she finds the headline she seeks:

MEAN STREETS
Cottoncroft Youth in Hospital after Vicious Attack

She reads the story:

A teenager was rushed to hospital on Saturday after he was set upon and beaten in Market Street. Joshua Winnifrith (pictured right) is sixteen and attends Cottoncroft Comprehensive School. He sustained four cracked ribs and a fractured collar-bone, plus bruises and abrasions. Delayed concussion caused Joshua to slur his words as he tried to tell our reporter what happened.

'It's all a bit hazy,' he said. 'I was on my way to work. One minute I was walking along, the next there were two men blocking my way. One of them said something — I don't remember his exact words — then they started in on me. I was thrown to the ground and kicked repeatedly. I must have passed out because the next thing I knew my attackers had gone and a passer-by was bending over me.'

A hospital spokesperson told our reporter she expected Joshua to remain in hospital for several days. The police have interviewed him, but had no comment to make at this stage.

That's it. No mention of the Flitcrofts. Nothing about the Push.

'Load of flaming rubbish.' She screws up the paper, hurls it into a corner. 'We were *winning*,' she hisses at her tearful reflection in the mirror. '*Would* have won easily if it wasn't for windy newspapers, windy *newsagents* and interfering parents.' She jerks a tissue out of the box on the dressing table and buries her face in it, wishing Jane and Penny were here to share her distress.

FIFTY-TWO

Penny Cockroft wakes at six as usual, remembers there's nowhere to go and groans. She reminds herself of all the mornings she's had to drag herself out of bed when all she wanted to do was turn over and go back to sleep. It ought to make her feel cosy knowing she can drift off again, especially since she can hear rain hitting the window, but it doesn't. Her mind's racing, that's the trouble. *What's happening about the papers? Is Mr Patel delivering them all himself? What happened at Jane's house last night, and Jill's, and the twins, not to mention the evening girls and the Sunday girls? Where's their dosh going to come from? And mine?*

She can't sleep, but she makes herself stay in bed and doesn't get to school till her usual time. It's still raining. She finds Jill and Jane in the terrapin doorway.

'Have you two got the –'

'Sack, yes,' they reply in unison, and Jill adds, 'Have you seen the *Target*?'

'No, why?'

'They printed about Josh getting attacked, but nothing about Push *or* the Flitcrofts. Not a sausage. Just when things seemed to be swinging our way, we're let down by windy newspapers and news*agents*.'

Penny grins briefly. 'Good line that, Jillo. Windy newspapers and news*agents*. You could make a bomb writing speeches.'

'Yeah, well – I could do with making a bomb doing *something*. We *all* could.'

'Hey, listen,' says Jane, 'it's not *completely* bad.'

Jill scowls at her. 'What you on about, you amoeba – *you're* usually the gang moaner.'

'Yes I know, but I was thinking in bed this morning.'

'Who wasn't?' mutters Penny.

'No, listen, it's good is this. We stop paying Push dosh, yeah?'

'Yeah.'

'And Froggy Flitcroft doesn't like it 'cause his income goes down.'

'Right.'

'So what does he do – he gets the Push to lean on Mr Patel, and Patel sacks us.'

'We *know*.'

'OK, so then we're out of work so we're *still* not

paying Push dosh, so all Froggy's done is cut off his nose to spite his ugly fizzog, see?'

'Hmmm.' Penny nods. 'Looked at that way, the result's the same *and* we're not being threatened, I can see that. Trouble is, Push action doesn't *usually* end in the victim getting the sack. It's more likely to end with the victim coughing up, especially now Froggy's bringing the heavies in.' She frowns. 'What we need's a *break*. Something new. Something we can go to the police with.'

Jill sighs, shakes her head. 'Never happen, Pen. They're too clever, got all the bases covered. Your mass movement was a nice try but I'm afraid it's not going to work, even with Hezzy on board.'

'Well,' murmurs Jane, 'I think it's too soon to tell. I reckon we're still in with a chance.' She smiles at Penny. 'My gran's always saying it's a funny old world. Maybe the break you mentioned is just around the corner, Pen.'

FIFTY-THREE

'Flitcroft Staff Services, Mavis speaking. How may I help you? . . . Yes he is, who shall I say? . . . One moment, Mr Green . . . Charles, for you. Mr Green.'

'Morning, Mr Green . . . In the pink, thanks. Your-self? . . . Good, good. Now what can I do for you? . . . Saturday? That's the day after tomorrow, isn't it? . . . No – ha, ha, you're *not* through to the talking calendar, Mr Green – I'm just consulting *my* calendar and yes, Saturday should be fine . . . No, no, when I say *should* I mean will. Saturday *will* be fine . . . *Four* playmates? No problem. Does it matter which . . . er . . . ? . . . Two of each, right . . . Over fifteen . . . *not* over fifteen, OK, I've got that. Where? . . . Yes, I'm writing it down . . . Yes I know it, Mr Green. Not the *house* of course, but I know the street . . . Eight o'clock? No worries . . . Yes of course I'll be careful, I'm *always* careful, that's how I've stayed in business sixteen years without having my collar felt. You can rest easy, Mr Green, it's as good as done . . . Yes. I certainly will. I'll look forward to that . . . Yes, you too, Mr Green. Bye.

'YESSSS!'

FIFTY-FOUR

Seven o'clock Friday evening, Biff Barraclough and Sparky Sparks walk into Sizzlers burger joint, take a table for four. The place is full of kids. Biff studies the menu, slides it across to his companion, sits gazing out the window. Anne Myers and Lois Baxter are sharing a table across the room. The darkness outside turns the window into a mirror. Biff picks out the girls' reflection and sees that they're staring across at him. He knew they would be.

The waiter approaches, pad and pencil poised. 'Yes, sir?'

'Hungry Giant cheese and baconburger,' grunts Sparky. 'Triple fries, regular coffee.'

The waiter jots down the order, looks at Biff. 'And for you, sir?'

Biff looks up at him. 'Temporary, right?'

'Sorry?'

'You. Temporary. Filling in for the regular guy.'

'Oh yes, that's right. I'm pool staff, filling in for Josh who's away. Know him do you, sir?'

'We've met.'

'He's in hospital.'

'I know, it was in the paper.' Shakes his head. 'It's come to something when a guy can't walk down the street without some bastard maiming him. Gimme the high-stack jawstretcher, jumbo fries, hold the salad.' He pulls a face. 'Can't understand why they put bleedin' salad with everything nowadays, trying to turn us all into rabbits.' The waiter jots, says thanks, turns away. Biff watches him leave, then cuts his eyes towards Anne and Lois who look away quickly.

He chuckles and Sparky says, 'What?'

'Those two think we're flipping superheroes. Makes the job a doddle.'

'We doing it now, or after we eat?'

'Now, might as well.' He stares across until one of the girls meets his eye, then jerks his head in a beckoning motion. He sees her cheeks go red as she whispers to her friend. They're both looking now. Biff repeats the invitation and Lois mouths a question, '*Us?*' He nods, indicates the two vacant seats. They stand and come over, carrying their drinks.

'Sit down, girls, me and Sparky've got like a proposition to put to you.'

'We know you, me and Lois,' says Anne, setting down her drink. 'We're Push.'

Biff nods as the girls settle themselves. 'I know. Clocked you at HQ Monday. You're Cassette, she's Email, right?'

'Yes. It was wicked how you handled old Froggy. We loved it.'

'Yeah, well.' Biff grins. 'Hates parting with his dosh, old Froggy. Gotta be hard with him. Bet *you're* not on a fortune.'

'We're *not*, considering what we bring in and the risks we take.'

Biff nods. 'It's always been the same. Listen.' He leans across the table. 'How'd you like to make some *real* dosh?'

'You mean like you got Monday night?'

'Similar, yeah. What d'you say?'

Lois hesitates, pulls a face. 'What would we have to do?'

Biff shakes his head. 'Nothing you'd need a university education to do, Email.'

'Yeah, but like *what*? I mean you said yourself Froggy don't like parting with his dosh. Must be something dangerous if he's offering big bucks.'

'Yes, and why *us*,' queries Anne, 'when there's you and your friend? If it pays that well, why aren't *you* doing it?'

'Why aren't we doing it?' Biff laughs out loud, causing everybody in the place to look. He leans forward again. 'See, Cassette, me and Sparky here're not the right *material* for this job. It's sort of specialized. Not hard, not dangerous, but specialized. All you have to do –' his voice drops to a whisper – 'is go to a party.'

'A *party*?'

'Ssssh!' He frowns a warning. 'Yes, a party, tomorrow night, and there's no catch. You won't be *delivering* anything to this party, just your two selves, and it's going to be a good one. Booze, grub, music – all free. Stuff if you want it, also free, *and* you get fifty quid each after. How can you lose?'

The men's food arrives. Biff smiles at Lois. 'Why don't you and Cassette go back to your table and think about it while me and Sparky eat? There's no pressure, but I think you'd have to be crazy to turn this one down. See you in a bit.'

The girls take their drinks back to their table and converse in low tones, casting frequent glances in their heroes' direction. Sparky bites a chunk out of his Hungry Giant and winks at Biff. 'Take it from me, old son, they're hooked.'

Biff nods, shaking the vinegar bottle over his fries. 'I know.'

FIFTY-FIVE

Monday, eight thirty-five. Maisie Malin in the terrapin doorway, looking across at the science block. Gordon Barraclough's on the corner he always occupies on Mondays, pocketing Push dosh slipped to him by kids who haven't joined the resistance. She's disappointed. With Hezzy on Pull's side she's hoped today might be different, though in what way she's not sure, and her disappointment is compounded when she notices one or two Pull members among the payers. She aches to intercept these backsliders, plead with them not to give in, but she knows what they'd say. '*It's all right for you, Malin. Mummy and*

Daddy have taken you out of the firing-line. You're not going to wind up in hospital like Josh Winnifrith, we are, so shove off and mind your own business.' Couldn't blame 'em either, but it depresses her to have to watch resistance starting to crumble. She's about to walk away when she spots Hezzy himself striding across the yard.

'Barraclough,' he barks as he approaches, 'gymnasium, lad, *now*!' And sweeps by, heading towards the far end of the block where Colin Day can be seen loitering. Maisie's heart leaps as Barraclough leaves his post and trudges, muttering, towards the main block, and when she hears the Head bark the same order at Day, it soars. Walking along the corridor at five to nine, she passes the gymnasium door and sees Longstaff, Day and Barraclough standing, spaced so they can't communicate, under the eagle eye of Dan Traynor, whom the kids call Circuit.

A mood of cautious optimism infects the hundred or so members of Pull in their various classes as the school day commences, and when morning break rolls round and the three collectors are obliged to report once more to the gym, the mood becomes one of fierce joy. Nothing has been said, but it is obvious to the student body that the Head and his staff have begun a clampdown on the school's Push contingent. It is true that no action has as yet been taken against Anne Myers or Lois Baxter, but the general feeling is that this will follow quite swiftly should it become necessary, and when neither girl shows any inclination to collect during the day's three breaks, Pull knows it can claim a partial victory. There's no celebration though. Every member has seen Josh Winnifrith's picture in the *Target*, and knows it might well be their turn tomorrow.

FIFTY-SIX

'For God's sake, our Jason, turn the volume down, or better still switch the bloody thing off altogether.'

'No!' As Lois makes a dive for the remote control, the child snatches it from the sticky sofa arm and hugs it to the front of his T-shirt, kicking out at his sister, yelling, 'Oh, Mam, *tell* her. She's spoiling my programme.'

Donna Baxter sticks her head round the kitchen door. 'Will you *give up*, our Lois – you've done nothing but bug that skriking kid since you got in.' Kneeling on the sofa ignoring her mother, Lois fends off her brother's flying feet with one hand, wrests the remote from his puny grasp with the other and switches off. The silence is destroyed at once by the child's enraged screech. Donna, dishmop in hand, launches herself at her daughter's back as Lois straightens up, knocking her down on top of the infant. As the pair struggle to disentangle themselves the woman hits out repeatedly with the dishmop, grunting in time with the blows. 'When – am – I – ever – going – to – get – a – bit – of – peace – and – quiet – in – this – house – I'm – sick – and – tired – of – your – endless – bloody – NOISE.'

'It's him,' gasps Lois, throwing up her arms to ward off the mop, 'gawping at rubbish all day long.'

'''T'isn't, Mam, it's *her*, the bossy cow.'

'It's *both* of you!' screams Donna. The mop handle snaps. She flings the useless implement across the room, grabs two fistfuls of her daughter's hair, yanks her off the child and dumps her on the threadbare carpet. 'Get up, our Lois,' she pants, 'get up, get out of this house and leave your brother in peace. I don't know why you're still here anyway – you *never* stop in at night.'

'I'm *poorly*, Mam.' Lois slumps to the floor, buries her face in her folded arms. 'It was that party, Saturday night.'

'Yes, well I'm not surprised, our Lois.' Fists on hips, glaring down at her daughter. 'Stopping out till nearly three, drinking and smoking heaven knows what, popping pills I shouldn't wonder. What we need's a *man* about the house, my girl. A *father*. You wouldn't go gallivanting –'

'A *man*?' Lois raises her head, nods. 'Oh yes, that's

what we need all right, a man. You should've been there Saturday, Mam, you could've had your pick of 'em.' She laughs, only it sounds like a bark. 'Too many for me and Anne. Queuing up they were, videocams at the ready. "*All you have to do is go to a party*," says Biff. "*No catch.*"' She shakes her head. 'Oh no, not flipping much.'

Donna's expression changes. She drops to one knee beside the weeping girl, touches her shoulder. 'Lois, what are you talking about, videocams, queuing up?'

On the sofa, Jason jeers, 'Ha ha ha, our Lois is crying. Diddums, Loisy-woi –'

'SHUT UP!' The little boy flinches, sticks his thumb in his mouth, rocks himself. Donna bends over her daughter. 'Lois, whose party *was* this? Who was there? Where was it?' Lois rolls her head from side to side on her arms. 'Can't say, Mum. Push business. Too late anyway. Too flipping *late*.'

FIFTY-SEVEN

'Oh hi, Julie, it's Donna . . . Not too bad thanks. You? . . . Good. Look, I was wondering . . . has your Anne mentioned last Saturday at all: that party they went to, or have you noticed anything unusual about her, behaviour wise, only our Lois . . . *moody*, you can say that again. She's been like a bear with a sore . . . yes, I *know* it's their age, Julie, but this is *different*. . . No listen, she was tormenting our Jason so I pulled her off him, threw her on the floor. Now I'd *expect* her to either slam out of the house or lock herself in her room, but she didn't. She says, "*I'm poorly, Mam*," and breaks down roaring. Now you know *that's* not our Lois. *Then* she says, "*It was that party Saturday night*." So *I* says, "yes, I expect it was all booze and dope and pills," *then* she starts going on about *men*. Men queuing up with videocams, she says, and when I ask her whose party it was and *where* it was, she goes, "*can't say – Push business*". And now she's locked herself in her room and I can't get a word out of her . . . Yes, videocams . . . Well, *ask* her, Julie, because I don't mind telling you *I'm* concerned . . . Well of *course* you are, any mother would be . . . Ah-ha. And, Julie – give us a ring back if . . . thanks. Talk to you later then. Bye.'

FIFTY-EIGHT

As Email's mother talks to Cassette's mother on the phone, Jill Hall pushes through the revolving door into the reception area of the *Target* building and sees a teenage girl sitting behind a black steel desk. The desktop supports a phone, a keyboard and a monitor. Beside it in a black steel planter stands a weeping fig, too vivid to be real. Jill recognizes the receptionist as a former pupil of Cottoncroft Comp but doesn't know her name. She approaches the desk.

'Yes, how may I help you?'

'How do I find Dudley West, please?'

'Would that be Dudley West the reporter?'

'Yes.'

'Is Mr West expecting you?'

'Uh . . . no. He interviewed a friend of mine in hospital.'

The girl's smile is brittle. 'Mr West interviews a lot of people's friends, doesn't mean they can come walking in here and see him just like that. Is it important?'

'It is to me.'

The girl sighs, lifts the receiver, punches a button. 'Newsroom, this is Reception. There's a little girl to see Mr West, no appointment. Says it's important.' She looks at Jill, mouths '*Name?*' Jill gives her name, the girl repeats it in a bored voice. 'Right, triffic, thanks.' She hangs up, looks at Jill. 'Mr West's free as it happens, must be your lucky day. Take the lift, press two. He'll be waiting.'

★

'Now then, young lady, what can I do for you?'
They're sitting in a small bare office, just two chairs
and the table that separates them. Dudley West is a
tubby, balding man in his forties. He seems kind.

'I'm a friend of Josh Winnifrith,' says Jill. 'You
interviewed him up the Infirmary.'

'*Did* I?' The reporter frowns, then nods. 'Oh yes I
remember – he's the laddie got beaten up, isn't he?
How's he getting along?'

'He's still in hospital but they say he's going to be
fine. He said . . . he told me and my friends you were
going to print something about Push and the Flitcrofts
but you *didn't*. That's why I've come.'

'Ah.' Dudley West sits back, gazes at his visitor.
'Your friend Josh told me some youngsters are refusing
to pay what he calls Push dosh, Jill. Are you one of
them?'

'Yes I . . . well I *was*, but I've got the sack so I'm
not working. Look.' She frowns at the man. 'Me and
my friends don't understand: if you *know* about Push
dosh and Froggy Flitcroft and everything that's going
on, how come you don't put it in the paper? You
could get him in jail, him and a lot of others but you
don't. Why *not*, Mr West?'

'Hmmm.' The reporter nods, says nothing. Jill can
see he's thinking. After a minute he says, 'I can understand why it seems strange to you and your friends,
Jill, but you see, newspapers have to be very, very

careful what they print.' He looks at her. 'Do you know what libel is?'

Jill nods. 'I think so. Is it when someone prints something about somebody and it isn't true?'

'That's right, except that it can *also* be libel if it *is* true but you can't *prove* it, and that's what we're up against here at the *Target* with regard to Push and the Flitcrofts. We *know* what's going on, it's gone on for years but there's never any proof. Take your friend for example: *I* know it was the Push beat him up. It's nearly *always* Push when somebody's attacked in this town, but you see, there were no witnesses. There was just your friend and the men who attacked him. Even if they were caught it'd be his word against theirs, and if the *Target* ran a piece saying they were Push and they were carrying out Flitcroft's orders, Charles Flitcroft would sue us for every penny we've got.' He shrugs, smiles. 'D'you see?'

'I s'pose.' She sighed. ''T'isn't fair though, is it, Mr West, them getting away with everything?'

'Indeed it's not, Jill.' The reporter looks at her. 'For what it's worth, I think you and your friends are very brave defying the Push, and if you think I might be able to help you at any time *without* committing libel, I hope you'll come to me. Take this.' He slides a small card across the table, stands up. 'I'm truly sorry I can't offer more. Come on, I'll walk you to the lift.'

FIFTY-NINE

The buzzer brings Blood's session on the cardiovascular system to an end. 'All right, Year Eleven, off you go. *Quietly*.'

''Bout bloody time,' grunts Kieran Billings, screeching his chair on the boards. 'Another minute and I'd have been snoring.'

Tony Harrison snickers. 'You know what *you* need, don't you?'

'No, what *do* I need, smeghead?' Harrison has refused to join Pull and Kieran doesn't like him.

'You need an easier way of getting dosh. Won't catch *me* vanning it down to wurzel-land every Saturday morning when I can make fifty quid enjoying myself.'

'Oh yeah?' Kieran is interested in spite of himself. 'So go on then – how d'you make fifty quid enjoying yourself?' It's breaktime and they're on the corridor, heading for the yard.

Harrison speaks quietly. 'Easy. I show up at a party.'

'Don't tell me,' growls Kieran. 'It's a Push deal, right? You show up at a party with a pocketful of tabs to sell and your cut's fifty quid unless there's a raid, in which case it's eighteen months.'

'No no, there's no catch. I show up clean, grab a few bevvies, enter into the spirit, money for jam.' He looks sidelong at Billings. 'Could be you, Saturday night.'

'How *could* it, you donkey, with me in wurzel-land? Anyway I don't buy it. Nobody pays a guy just to go to a party. There's got to be something else.'

'Well, OK.' Harrison nods. 'There's *something*, but it's no big deal. Few drinkie-poos inside you, you don't notice, and if you do you don't care.' He grins. 'Come on spud-lifter, loosen up. Chuck a sickie and give it a go. What you got to lose?'

Kieran shrugs, pulls a face. He dislikes Harrison and he's not the party type, but the prospect of a lie-in Saturday morning is tempting and fifty quid is more than he'll clear chopping leeks. On the other hand, Harrison's evasive on what you do for the dosh, plus Kieran's pretty sure there's Push involvement somewhere. He nods, grunts, 'I'll think about it,' and lengthens his stride, leaving the other boy behind.

SIXTY

Charles Flitcroft pays for his half of bitter and carries it to the corner table where the man he knows as Mr Green sits waiting. It is nine o'clock Tuesday evening and The Adelphi bar is just busy enough to make them inconspicuous among the sales reps and transients who will be staying the night at the hotel. Charles sets down his glass on a beermat, lowers himself on to a padded stool and nods.

'Mr Green.'

'Flitcroft.' In front of Green is a whisky glass and a trade magazine, folded. 'When you leave, pick up the magazine. Don't unfold it till you're in your car.'

'Thanks. How was it, Saturday?'

'I wasn't there myself but I'm told it went well.'

'I'm glad. What about *next* Saturday? Same?'

Green shakes his head. 'Rule number one: never the same twice running.' He lifts the whisky glass, sips, sets it down. 'Old and valued client, recently moved to Cottoncroft. Can you oblige?'

'Of course. Two pairs again?'

'Yes. You'll find the address with your cash. It's five K by the way, as agreed.'

'Fine.' Froggy licks his lips, shakes his head. 'You represent a prosperous concern, Mr Green.'

Green hears the greed in the man's voice, nods. 'It's all down to the Internet, Flitcroft. A simple transaction here in Cottoncroft generating trade around the planet.' He chuckles, though his eyes don't smile. 'Demand for our product is colossal, and it's not easily available everywhere.'

Charles looks at him. 'I suppose not. Er . . . do I see you here a week today?'

'Certainly not.' Green drains his glass, sets it down. 'Never the same twice running, remember?' He leans forward, murmurs, 'Patterns get noticed, Flitcroft. They attract attention. Secret of a long and happy career is to avoid making 'em. I'll call you.' He stands up and walks away. Flitcroft sits sipping his bitter, curbing his impatience to be riffling through large coarse banknotes. A pleasure postponed is a pleasure enhanced, as his old granny never used to say. His free hand lies lightly along the glossy cylinder of the magazine. He looks cool, but inside is a glow of fierce pride as he surveys the other customers over the rim of his glass. How surprised they'd be if they knew they shared this bar with a big-time operator; a guy who makes more on a single Saturday night than most of them earn in a month. A phrase springs to mind; an apt phrase. *The Al Capone of Cottoncroft.* Charles likes it. He smiles.

SIXTY-ONE

'Can I have a word, Sand?' Wednesday morning, ten to nine. Sandra shackles her bike, shakes her head.

'Wasting your breath, Cassette. I'm not paying.'

''Tisn't about that. Well it is sort of, but –'

'Listen.' Sandy straightens up. 'Are you so thick, Anne Myers, that you haven't noticed things have changed around here? Where're Barraclough, Long-staff and Day? Standing in the gym, that's where. And why? Because Hezzy's on to 'em, and if he's on to *them*, he's on to you as well, so if I were you . . . here, what's *up*?'

Anne wipes her cheek with the back of a hand, shakes her head, sniffles. 'I'm not after Push dosh, Sand, I wanna tell you something.' Her voice is shaky. Sandra frowns.

'Getting *scared* are we, now that things're starting to go wrong?'

'No!' Anne shakes her head. 'It's *not* that.' She glances about, lowers her voice. 'Something hap-pened, Saturday night. I want Pull to know about it, but Fax and them mustn't know I grassed.'

'Huh?' Sandy stares at the girl. 'Are you saying you want to *help* us . . . Pull, I mean?'

Anne nods. 'Yeah.'

Sandy's eyes narrow. 'Why're you switching sides, Cassette? Your mates *murder* someone or what?'

'No, it's not murder but it's bad and I'm sure Froggy Flitcroft's at the back of it. Listen.' Her voice drops to a hiss. 'We met these two guys in Sizzlers, Friday night. Biff and Sparky, and they said did we want to make some serious dosh. Me and Lois, this was. All we had to do was show up at a party . . .'

SIXTY-TWO

'John, have you got a minute?' Morning break.

Twenty-a-side soccer on the field, no ref, Passmore in goal. Somebody volleys from six yards out. Ball curls towards the top corner, Passmore leaps, tips it over, glances at Sandy behind the posts. 'Does it look like it?'

An opponent places the ball for the corner. Thirty-eight bodies pack the goal mouth. Passmore skips and cranes for a view of the kick. 'It's pretty urgent, John.'

It's a high one, arcing over a sea of heads, dropping towards the far post. Passmore, eye on the ball, barges into team-mates and opponents, makes it his, clutching it to his chest. 'It better be, Sand.' He grabs a boy's sleeve. 'Take over, Lee, will you?' Leaves the pitch, falls in step beside the girl. 'What?'

'Anne Myers came up to me before school, told me something.'

'Something?'

'Something bad, but good in a way I think. Good for Pull.'

The boy stops. 'Bad, good – what the heck're you *talking* about, Sand?'

Sandra looks at him. 'You know we've been saying we need a break – something we can go to the police with?'

'Yeah?'

'Well, I think we've got it.'

'You *do*? Why, what's she said?'

'It's about a party she and Lois were at, Saturday night.'

'A party – what's *that* got to do with anything, Sand?'

Sandy pulls a face. 'It wasn't the usual sort of party, John. They were offered dosh to be there, and there were men.'

'Men?'

'Yeah, men with videocams, taking shots.'

'Shots of *what*?'

'Well . . .' Sandy feels her cheeks burn. 'Thing is,

Anne says they gave 'em booze, got them tipsy, then
. . . then made them take their kit off.'

'What?' Passmore looks incredulous. 'A *strip*-party,
you mean?'

Sandy shakes her head. 'Worse than that. Look, it's
hard for me to talk about this, John, it's embarrassing.'

'Aaah.' The boy's face clears and he nods, slowly.
'If . . . if you're saying what I think you're saying,
Sand, you were right just now. It's bad – probably
the worst thing old Froggy's been involved in if he *is*
involved, and it could be exactly what we need to
put him on the spot, but only if we've got *proof.* D'you
think Anne'd tell the police what she told you?'

'No way – she *said* nobody must know she grassed.'
She stands, hands in pockets, gazing across the field.
'And anyway that wouldn't be proof. What we
need –' she laughs briefly – 'what we need is one of
the videocams, complete with pics of Cassette and
Email in the nude. Now *that's* what I call proof.'

'Well yes,' Passmore kicks a tussock, 'in an ideal
world, but you know and I know that those cams
could be anywhere by now, *and* the guys that used
'em.' He sighs theatrically. 'Shame it wasn't *you* got
the invitation, Sand.'

'Thanks a flipping *bunch*!' growls Sandy.

'No, but just think . . .'

'I *know*.' Sandy nods. 'He'd have been finished, but
he's not daft enough to recruit someone from Pull.

Still –' she shakes her head – 'I can't help thinking the break we've been hoping for is in this party thing somewhere, if we can only find it.'

As the buzzer goes and they move towards the main block, Passmore shakes his head. 'Y'know, Sand, I'm not at all sure we've the right to keep this "*party thing*" as you call it, to ourselves.'

'How d'you mean?'

'Well – suppose there's another? Shouldn't we *tell* somebody so girls can be warned? You've got to admit it's a point.'

Sandy shakes her head. 'There won't be another, John.'

'There *might* be. Anyway, think about it. We'll talk later.'

'Yeah, John. Later.'

SIXTY-THREE

Lunch. Kieran Billings opts for the steak pie and chips with a strawberry yogurt to follow, picks up his tray, looks around. Tony Harrison's sharing a corner table with one guy but there's two empty chairs between them. Safe enough if you don't shout. He goes across, plonks down the tray, sits. 'Tony.'

'Oh hi, spud-lifter.' Harrison grins. 'Been thinking about my suggestion, have you?'

'Yeah.' Kieran picks up his fork, jabs at the slab of pie. 'Where do I meet you, *if* I decide to come?'

Harrison shakes his head. 'It's not like that, I won't be going. You'll need to talk to my cousin. He's setting it up.'

'Who's your cousin?'

'You don't know him. Sparky Sparks. Hangs around Sizzlers.'

'What's he look like?'

'You don't have to know that. If you're serious I'll call him up, describe *you*.'

'How would I get paid?'

'Sparky'll tell you that. Want me to call him or not? I've got the mobile.'

'Uh . . . yeah, all right.'

'You'll go tonight?'

'You said Saturday.'

'Not the *party*, you donkey. *Sizzlers*.'

'Oh – oh yeah.'

'What time?'

'Eight o'clock?'

'OK. Mobile doesn't work too good in here so I'll go on the field.' He winks. 'More private anyway.' He pushes back his chair, stands up.

'Hang on a minute, I've got a question.'

'What?'

'Why're you doing this – what's in it for you?'

'Me?' Wide-eyed innocence. 'I'm giving my cousin a hand, that's all. Nothing in it for me.'

'Yeah, right.' Kieran's eyes narrow. 'And Push – where do *they* fit in?'

'Push?' Harrison shakes his head. 'Nowhere that I know of.' He gazes at the other boy. 'You are *sure* about this aren't you, spud-lifter? Only once I call Sparky, you're in.' He leers. 'Sparky's not crazy about time-wasters. *Crazy*, yes, but not about guys who don't show up, so you *will* go?'

'I *said* so. Go make your call.'

Harrison leaves. Kieran watches him go, then pokes at his pie, thinking, *Fifty quid's fifty quid and sleeping late for once'll be mega, but I'm not sure it's that smart, what I'm doing. Wish there was someone I could talk to about it . . .*

SIXTY-FOUR

Three-thirty. John Passmore catches Sandy as she and Beryl mount their bikes. 'Thought I'd let you know what I've decided.'

'What – the party thing?'

'Yes. Does she . . . ?' He indicates Beryl.

'I've told her about Anne, yes.'

'Right. Well, what I thought was, we won't go to Hezzy or anybody for the moment, but we could put up a notice saying something like, "*Any girl getting an unexpected party invitation should see Sandra Lister or John Passmore before attending. This is vitally important.*" What d'you think?'

Sandy pulls a face. 'Push're going to know somebody squealed, and it could only be Anne or Lois. I'm not sure, John.'

Beryl snorts. 'Anne and Lois aren't the only ones risking a doing, Sand. It could be you and me tonight, for not paying.' She turns to Passmore. 'Put it up and let 'em take their chance, John – they've dished it out often enough.'

Passmore arches his brows. 'OK with you, Sand?'

Sandy shrugs. 'Outvoted, aren't I? Go for it.'

'I'll run it up on the processor tonight, post it first thing. See you.'

The two girls watch him depart. 'One of the good guys, old John,' murmurs Beryl. 'How many Year Twelves do *you* know who'd clear something with a couple of Year Elevens before going ahead?'

Sandy grins. 'I don't know *any*, Bez, but I think I know a Year Eleven who's got the hots for a certain Year Twelve.' She ducks and accelerates away as her friend swings her backpack at her head.

SIXTY-FIVE

He pins up the notice between the changing rooms and is heading for the yard when he hears his name called and turns to see a Year Eleven stumbling after him. Scruffy-looking guy, always seems half asleep. *Billings*, that's the name. 'Yes?'

'That notice – what's it mean?'

He scowls at the boy. 'It's not addressed to *you*, Billings, unless you're a heavily disguised girl.'

'No, listen, what's this about parties, 'Cause *I've* had an invitation and *it* was unexpected.'

'*You?*' Passmore laughs. 'I don't think they'd invite you to the sort of party that notice is about, Billings.'

'You don't know. Mine's one you get dosh for.'

'What?'

'Dosh. I've been promised fifty quid for showing up at a party; fifty quid and all the booze I can handle.'

'*Who*, Billings? Who promised you?'

'Don't know if I ought to tell you that, only I'm worried. Haven't slept all night, probably give backword today if I wasn't shit-scared of Sparky.'

'Hold on a sec, let's go in here.' Passmore takes the lad's elbow, steers him into the boys' changing room, back-heels the door shut. 'Now, who promised you dosh . . . er . . . what's your first name?'

'Kieran.'

'Who promised you, Kieran? It's vital you tell me. Serious crime, girls at risk, stuff like that. You could end up inside.'

'*Me?* All *I've* done is –'

'So *tell* me.'

'Harrison. Tony Harrison. He's *been* to one, says it's dosh for jam.'

'Was Email there, and Cassette?'

'I dunno, he didn't mention it, just said it was easy money that's all.'

'And who's this Sparky you're scared of?'

'Guy I met last night at Sizzler's, built like a tank. Harrison's cousin. He gave me the address, other details, told me he'd rip my head off and pee down the inside of my neck if I blabbed, so here I am blabbing.'

Passmore shook his head. 'Don't worry –'

'*Be happy*, yes I know, I've heard it.'

'No listen. You know Pull's desperate to get something on Froggy Flitcroft don't you, Kieran?'

'Sure. De-mythologization, Gary Waterhouse calls it. I told him I'd join in when *he'd* de-mythologized a few of Froggy's mates.'

'Yes, well, I think Froggy's got something to do with this party you're going to, and if you're up for it you might *just* be the guy who puts him where he belongs. Him and a few more. What d'you say?'

'Well . . . depends what I'd have to *do*. I mean, I'd sort of like to hang on to my head if it's all the same to you.'

Passmore pulls a face. 'I'm not sure how we'd handle it, Kieran, not yet. I'll need to talk to some people, get back to you.' He gazes at the boy. 'We'll want you to go to the party as agreed though, if that's all right?'

Kieran shrugs. 'Like I told Gary Waterhouse, it's the Gangmasters I'd like to bust, but I suppose I could give it a go if it's not too risky.'

Passmore nods grimly. 'You could try looking at it this way, Kieran. From what you've said about Sparky I'd say you're committed to the party anyhow, and if it's the sort of party I think it'll be you'll be better off as a saboteur than a victim.'

'Victim?' Kieran looks at him. 'That bad, huh?'

'If what Anne Myers says is true, yes.'

'Jeez.'

'Absolutely. Anyway,' John glances at his watch, 'we'd better split before buzzer. You go now, I'll follow.' *Girls and boys*, he thinks as Billings departs. *Kinkier and kinkier.*

SIXTY-SIX

Six o'clock. Dark already on a cold, drizzly evening. Twins Clare and Nikki Mortimer hunch along the rain-slick pavement, hoods up, hands in pockets, heading for the bright lights and loud company of Sizzlers burger joint. They haven't a lot of time and almost no money, but they're fed up of sitting in the house every night, gawping at the telly.

At this hour the place is almost empty. They choose a table by the window, shuck off their wet puffers, hang them on chairbacks. Nikki studies the menu, Clare looks round the room. Two kids she doesn't know, two guys in a corner, a bag-lady making a coffee spin out, that's it. She sighs. Maybe kids'll show up in a bit.

A waiter approaches. 'What can I get you, girls?'

Nikki looks at her sister. 'How much you got?'

Clare snaps open her purse, peers in. 'Two thirty I think, no, two thirty-three. You?'

'One eighty-eight.' She looks at the ceiling, adding up in her head. The waiter sighs. Nikki looks at him. 'We've got four twenty-one between us, what can we get?'

He shakes his head. 'We've nothing for two ten, so you'd have to share.'

'OK, let's see.' The twins put their heads together over the menu. The waiter sighs again, says he'll come back when they've decided, moves away.

'Bit stretched are we, girls?' Startled, they look up. Clare recognizes one of the guys from the corner. He grins down at them, hands in pockets.

'Pardon?'

'Bit stretched. You know – short of the old readies?'

'Oh . . . oh yeah, we lost our jobs.'

'Jobs?' The man's eyebrows rise. 'How old are you?'

'Fourteen. We're twins.'

'Yes, I noticed. So you're still at school then?'

'Oh yes, I didn't mean *proper* jobs. We had paper-rounds.'

'Ah well, never mind. What d'you fancy?'

'How d'you mean?'

'To eat. Tell me what you fancy and I'll pick up the tab. My pleasure.'

'No.' Clare shakes her head. 'Thanks. We don't take dosh from strangers.'

The man laughs. 'Won't be dosh, will it – just grub.'

'Don't take that either.'

'Don't take *anything*,' confirms Nikki. 'We're not daft.'

'Look.' The man lays big hands flat on the table,

leans in. 'I hear what you're saying and I'm with you, one hundred per cent. You can't be too careful these days, but all I'm doing is standing two girls who're down on their luck a burger. It's no big deal.'

'Yes, well thanks all the same, but we'd rather pay our way.' Nikki turns to Clare. 'What we having, sis?' Shutting him out.

'OK.' The man holds up his hands, palms towards them. 'You're right, people should pay their way, but it's not easy with no job, is it? You'll be looking for work, I suppose?'

'Course.' *Why doesn't he buzz off? Maybe I should complain to the waiter.*

'It just so happens I know someone – a lady – who's on the lookout for two smart girls like you.'

Clare glances up at him, sighs. 'To do *what?*'

The man shrugs. 'Bit of waitressing, that's all. Posh party.'

'What, you mean just *once?*'

'Well, yes, but good dosh. Very good in fact.'

'What d'you call good?' Clare is interested in spite of herself.

'Fifty.'

'Fifty *pounds? Each?*

'Yep. I told you, it's a posh do. Are you interested?'

'Well . . .' She looks at her twin. 'What d'you reckon, sis?'

Nikki shrugs. 'We've no experience. She could

get experienced waitresses for fifty quid, couldn't she?'

The man chuckles. 'Of *course* she could, but that's not what she wants. Professional waitresses . . . well, they tend to be *hard*, you know? Seen it all before. *Slapdash* is the word I'm groping for, I think. This lady wants young, fresh-faced girls. Girls who'll *smile* as they walk round with the nibbles, the drinkie-poos. And *twins*.' He smiles broadly. 'I should think she'll just about die of happiness when she sees you two. Look.' He produces a bit of lined notepaper, unfolds it, smooths it on the tabletop. 'This is where she lives . . .'

SIXTY-SEVEN

Mavis Flitcroft sits in the swivel chair, gazing through the window at passers-by on Manchester Road. It's Friday and a murky morning, but the strained look on the woman's face isn't due to the weather. When her husband bustles through with a sheaf of printouts she says, 'It's time to bale out, Charles.'

'Hmmm . . . what?' Absently, dropping the printouts in the mail tray.

'I said it's time to bale out.'

He stops, scowls at her. 'Bale out, what the devil do you mean? Bale out of what?'

She sighs. 'Listen, Charles, this firm – Flitcroft Staff Services – doesn't do too badly, certainly better than a lot of small businesses these days, and we've got just about everything we want. I'd be easier in my mind if we ran the agency and dropped all this other stuff.'

'Oh, you *would*?' Charles glares at his wife. 'So the fifteen years I've grafted building up what you call "*all this other stuff*" has been a waste of time, has it?' He snorts. 'What about the white Merc, Mavis – you've enjoyed cruising round town in that, and Flitcroft Staff Services didn't pay for it – *all this other stuff* did. All your little luxuries – every one of them – is financed out of the deals *I* make in this town. Goddam it, I *am* Cottoncroft. Nothing goes down here that I don't know about. No deal I don't take my cut. I'm *feared*, Mavis, and when you're feared you don't need to be *liked*, don't have to worry about *respectability*.' He turns from her to gaze out the window, hands in pockets, breathing hard.

Mavis speaks quietly to her husband's back. 'If I gave a damn about respectability, Charles, I'd have walked out on you years ago. I'm suggesting we go legitimate *not* so I can feel respectable in my old age, but so we stay out of jail.' She shivers. 'I've got used to my little luxuries, I'd be dead in a month in Holloway.'

Charles turns to face her. '*Holloway?* Why are you

talking about Holloway all of a sudden? Just because there's been a little glitch – because a bunch of kids decide to get stroppy, you start going on about –'

Mavis shakes her head. 'Can't you *see*, Charles, it's not a little glitch any more. It's not just *kids*. Tate's involved. You know – the Head up the Comp. The police are sniffing round since your ape-men crippled that waiter, and you choose a time like this to get into that dodgy deal with Green.' She shakes her head again. 'Error of judgement, Charles. Everything's escalating, snowballing, I haven't slept for a week. It's not too late if we drop it now, but if we don't they'll have us, and sooner rather than later.'

'Rubbish!' Charles's face is scarlet with fury, his eyes bulge as though he's about to blow himself to bits. 'Error of judgement. Don't you tell *me* I've made an error of judgement, you silly bitch. There's nothing wrong with *my* judgement, it's *yours* if you think you can have everything I've given you and not accept an element of risk. I don't *make* errors, Mavis, that's how I got where I am today.' He sticks out his chest, puffed up like a bullfrog. 'The Al Capone of Cottoncroft, they call me.' Catching sight of his reflection in the window he smiles broadly. 'Yeah, that's it, the Al Capone of Cottoncroft.'

SIXTY-EIGHT

Lunchtime. In the gym, CD, Fax and Walkman stand sullen on their white lines. In the cafeteria, second sitting is underway. John Passmore has commandeered a corner of the Year Twelve common room and is talking quietly to eight younger kids who shouldn't really be there.

'So what we're looking at here is a breakthrough: a chance to damage Froggy Flitcroft so badly he'll be finished in Cottoncroft. Kieran here's been invited to a party, and I have it from no less an authority than the former Dot Com that the guy who invited him is a Push operative.' He nods towards Kieran who seems to be asleep, but who lifts his shaggy head and grins round the company before dozing off again. Passmore smiles ruefully. 'He might not *look* much, but Kieran's agreed to –'

''Scuse me.'

John breaks off, recognizes the girl who interrupted Hezzy the other day, sighs. 'Yes, Penelope?'

'You said Kieran's been invited to a party?'

'That's right, but we're not talking about your average Saturday night bash. I was about to explain –'

'It's just . . . Clare and Nikki are off to a party too. Waitressing.' Penny breaks off, cheeks flaming. 'Sorry, I didn't mean to . . .'

Passmore nods. ''s OK, Penelope, no problem.' She subsides and he continues. 'Kieran's agreed to show up at this party and act for Pull, which is important because as I've said, we're not talking about your average party.'

His audience listens raptly as he tells them about Anne Myers, how she and Lois Baxter were approached at Sizzlers and offered money to attend a party. He's about to go on to the men and their digicams when Penny jumps up. 'That's where Clare and Nikki were, Sizzlers. This man came up to them –'

'Hang on.' John Passmore lifts a hand, stopping her. 'You say they were approached at Sizzlers?'

'Yes. Guy says he can get them work, waitressing at a posh party Saturday night. Fifty quid each.'

'What's the guy's name?'

Penny shrugs. 'Dunno, you'd have to ask them.'

Passmore nods. 'Don't worry, I will. Did they agree to go?'

'What do *you* think – fifty quid.'

He shakes his head. 'They'd earn it, Penelope, and not for taking trays round. Tell 'em I want to talk to them after school, will you? It's desperately important.'

'OK.'

John continues. When he's finished, Maisie Malin frowns. 'How do we know these parties have anything to do with Froggy, John?'

'I told you, Maisie, Dorothy Comstock. I'd a hunch this Sparky who approached Kieran at Sizzlers might be Push so I ran his name by Dorothy, who can't do enough bad turns for her old mates since they ditched her. She confirms Sparky's Push. If he's recruiting kids for dodgy parties, he's doing it for Froggy.'

Maisie grins, sits back. 'So it's practically in the bag, eh? Beautiful.'

John pulls a face. 'Not in the bag, Maisie, not yet. We're up against ruthless people, and it's a dangerous game Kieran's going to be playing.' He looks round. 'Can you all come back here after school?'

Everybody can. John reminds Penny to bring the twins. The meeting breaks up. Kieran stretches, yawns, stands. Kids are trooping out of the room, watched by resentful Year Twelves.

In the lounge bar of the Cross Keys, the Al Capone of Cottoncroft is enjoying a pint and a sandwich. If he knew what was brewing up at the Comprehensive, his appetite would be a bit less keen.

SIXTY-NINE

'What are you going to use for *money*?' asks the twins' mother as Nikki and Clare come downstairs in their party kit. It's seven o'clock, Saturday.

'It's a *party*, Mum,' laughs Clare, though she's never felt less like laughing. 'You don't *buy* the grub at a party.'

Their mother pulls a face. 'No, of course you don't. It's just . . . I know I'm being silly, darlings, but I wish you weren't going. You hear of such *awful* things happening to young people nowadays. Ecstasy, *draw*, whatever that is . . .'

'Aw, Mu-um, we're not *daft*. We won't get into drugs. Just dancing, a few drinks, a laugh with our friends. Nothing to worry about.'

'Mothers *do* worry though, darlings. They can't help it.' She looks from one to the other. 'Promise me you won't stay *too* late – I shan't sleep a wink till you're both home safe and sound.'

'We promise, Mum.'

'Thank you.' She smiles. 'You look absolutely terrific, the pair of you. Off you go, and have a fabulous time.'

'God!' groans Nikki as they set off down the street. 'That was *awful*. I nearly burst out crying when she said "*I shan't sleep a wink . . .*"'

'I *know*, I was the same. I kept thinking, *we don't have to do this. We can stop in, stay safe. It's the police's* job to catch Froggy Flitcroft. . . And hasn't the *day* dragged?'

'Hoo – you can say *that* again. It's felt like a fortnight.'

They stand by the bus stop. Nobody else is waiting. Clare peers along the road. 'How long?'

Nikki glances at her watch. 'Should be along in four minutes.' She looks down, screwing the sole of her shoe into the pavement. 'I'm scared, sis.'

Clare snorts. 'D'you think *I'm* not? I never thought I'd get involved in something like this in my whole life. It's the sort of stuff you see on the telly.'

'Yeah, well – let's hope the good guys show up in the nick of time like they do on the telly.'

Nikki shivers. And to think when I was younger I used to *pray* for a real-life adventure. Tipping back her head she peers into the void beyond the street-lamp's orange glow. 'Are you there, God? I was joking before. D'you think I could have a pizza and an early night instead? I'll never ask for anything again . . .'

SEVENTY

At 10 Givenham Place, all is ready. Linton Winters takes a final look round the room. On the walnut sideboard his mother used to polish daily, stand plates and bowls of party food. At intervals round the walls are occasional tables laden with bottles, decanters, glasses; all twinkling under the soft influence of indirect lighting. At one end of the room the solid cube of greenish glass he has for a coffee table holds a silver cigarette-box, a jasperware table lighter and a number of smaller boxes containing pills and powders specially delivered last night from an address in Back Quebec Street. The other end of the room is occupied by a velvet-upholstered sofa, a chaise-longue and a few armchairs. Cushions and beanbags lie plumply on the thick Chinese carpet. In a corner a CD player leaks Mozart into the warm, scented air.

Satisfied, he turns and trips lightly down a flight of carpeted stairs and along the hallway to the front door. He flicks the porchlight switch, opens the door and stands on the step inhaling cool night air, rubbing his large hands together, watching for the playmates.

There has been a serious shortage of playmates in Linton's life. His plainness made him invisible at school and this carried over into his teenage years. He found it difficult to persuade girls to go out with him. When girls did make dates, they either failed to show up or refused to repeat the experience. While others courted, married and started families, Linton lived with his mum, shopping for her after work, eating the meals she cooked, wearing the old-fashioned woollies she knitted for him. The old lady died in 1989, disappointed at her only son's failure to give her grandchildren. Linton was forty.

Lonely, he looked for a hobby and found photography. He bought the right tackle, learned developing and printing, made monochrome studies from nature. He'd joined a local camera club and through it he met and got talking to Gordon Staples, another loner who'd taken up photography as a way of meeting people. The major difference between them was that Gordon was not interested in nature shots; at least not the sort Linton was taking. It was some weeks before he told Linton about his particular speciality, and some weeks more before he invited his friend round to his place and showed him some prints. 'Beautiful, aren't they?' he breathed, as Linton gazed at them. 'And the beauty of it is, they sell.' He chuckled. 'This is just a hobby, but I don't need the day job any more. It's a beard, that's all.'

'Beard?' Linton whispered, without taking his eyes off the soft-focus print he was studying.

'Yes. You know – something you wear to hide your true identity.' Gordon chuckled again. 'Wouldn't do for all and sundry to know where my *real* dosh comes from, would it?'

'I suppose not,' croaked his guest, 'but how the heck d'you get *models*. I mean, your average mum isn't going to bring little Wendy to the studio to have *this* sort of snap done, is she?'

Gordon smiled, shook his head. 'Ways and means, Linton, ways and means.' He regarded the other man narrowly. 'Why – interested, are you?'

His guest nodded. '*More* than. I didn't know . . . I've been looking for something like this all my life. How do I . . . ?'

'Easy,' murmured Gordon, 'I vouch for you – your discretion and all that – and you're in. I take it you *are* discreet?'

'Oh, absolutely.'

Now, two years and more little models than he can count later, Linton stands at the front door of his new home, waiting for his latest quartet and the handful of discreet friends who will film them. Well, no, not *film*, strictly speaking. The march of technology has brought the videocam, which captures the image electronically without the need for film, and can transmit it via a capture-box directly on to the Internet. He smiles. Three or four hours from now, clips of this evening's revels will be viewed by connoisseurs on the other side of the world. Appetites will be whetted. Mouths will water. Orders will be placed.

Ah, see — here come the first pair, passing through the amber puddle from a streetlight. Sisters? Could almost be twins, now that would be a bonus. They're counting numbers, the little sweethearts. Number six, number eight . . . yes, here it is, darlings, you've found it. He steps into the light, a smile of welcome on his lips.

SEVENTY-ONE

The man who ushers Clare and Nikki indoors doesn't know he's watched from behind a skip by seven pairs of eyes. He follows the twins upstairs, leaving the door open. John Passmore nods to Kieran Billings. 'Better go, Kieran — girls'll feel better if you're with 'em. Good luck.' Kieran smiles wanly, straightens up and crosses the road. The others, crouched in the shadow of the skip, follow with their eyes. As Kieran reaches the gateway of number ten a boy approaches from the other direction and follows him up the path. John shoots an inquiring glance at Maisie Malin, who shrugs. 'Don't know him.'

'Photographer?' suggests Lauren.

'Nah.' John shakes his head. 'Too young. Kieran's partner, more like.'

As the boys reach the open door, the man reappears, invites them to cross the threshold and follows them inside. As he does so a black Mondeo cruises into view and pulls over a few metres beyond the house. Lamplight illuminates the bottom half of the driver's face leaving the top half in shadow. He sits a moment, then gets out and hurries with his head down and his hands in his pockets through the gateway.

'*That's* a photographer,' breathes John.

Ten minutes crawl by while the watchers wonder how Kieran and the twins are coping. Then a second car comes scrunching into view and parks in deep shadow. Two men get out. The friends draw back behind the skip. The men stride up the path of number ten, knock softly and are admitted.

Five minutes. Eight. Ten. Maisie sighs. 'Small party, three guys.'

John shakes his head. 'No, look.' Two cars, bumper to bumper, showing no lights. They draw up under some sycamores. After a minute three men come quickly towards number ten, glancing about them as though nervous.

'Six,' murmurs Jill.

Penny nods. 'Plus the host. Hope none of them're armed.'

'Oooh, don't say *that*,' shivers Jane. 'Scary enough as it is.'

'Armed with digicams,' growls John. 'Nothing else.' He hopes he's right.

An old man appears with a small dog on a lead. The six youngsters flatten themselves against the skip. As the man draws level the dog starts tugging at the lead, growling, trying to get at the people its nose says are there. The six hold their breath but the old man's yank on the lead almost pulls the dog off its feet. 'Come on, you daft bugger, we haven't got all night.' Penny stifles a yelp of mirth. Dog and master shuffle off round a curve.

Five minutes go by. A few cars have passed, none has stopped. 'D'you think that's it?' asks Maisie.

John shrugs. 'Who knows, best wait a bit.'

Five more minutes, no new arrivals. John turns. 'OK, that seems to be it. Got the plasticine, Maisie?'

'Yes.' She shrugs off her backpack, sets it on the ground, unfastens it.

'Right. Four cars, plus one up the side of the house makes five. Five lumps please, Maisie.'

'Coming up.' Maisie has produced some flat cardboard packets from her backpack. She deals them out like cards. Eager fingers tear them open, pull out the strips of plasticine, dump the packets in the skip. They scrunch the strips, knead them into soft warm balls. When that's done, John nods.

'Right. Give me yours, Jane, and yours, Penny. You're our snoopers. Lauren, you take the Mondeo. Jill, the Golf. Maisie, you'll do the Merc, and I'll see to the Audi and whatever that wreck is beside the house. Off you go, snoopers.'

Jane walks to where the road curves. Penny goes the other way, stops under a lamp. Both signal all clear. 'Go!' barks John and they run, the four of them, towards their designated vehicles.

SEVENTY-TWO

The twins stand either side of the kingsize bed, gazing at the outfits Linton Winters has laid out for them on the duvet. They are recognizable as the sort of uniform you see on waitresses in old movies, but these are shiny with wear and the skirts are far too brief. Nikki gulps.

'Are we really gonna put these *on*, sis?'

Clare pulls a face. 'I suppose.' She starts to unbutton her top. Nikki hasn't moved. Clare looks at her. 'Come on, love, at least we *knew* it wasn't going to be a waitressing job. Think how we'd be feeling if –'

'I'd be walking out, sis. *Running* out. I *know* we

knew, but I can't go through there wearing this . . . tat. How would Mum feel?'

'Mum'll never *know*, Nikki, and think – it means nobody'll have to wear it again, *ever*.' She sighs. 'We promised, everybody's relying on us, so come on.'

In an adjacent room, Kieran and a boy called Sam Bramley from the City Tech have wriggled into a pair of outrageously tight flunkey suits. Bramley stares at his reflection in the full-length mirror on the back of the wardrobe door. 'Jesus, I don't know if I can show my face in this kit even for fifty quid, and I'm *definitely* not wearing that wig. What sort of weirdos're coming to this party anyway?'

Kieran gazes at him. 'What did they tell you when they recruited you, Sam?'

Sam shrugs. 'Guy said they wanted waiters for a posh party, but I didn't think he meant *this* posh. We're like extras in that flipping George the Third film. I've a good mind to tell the geezer he can stuff it.'

'Don't, please.'

'Why not? You can do the same. He can't *make* us go through with it.'

Kieran shakes his head. 'Look, Sam, there's something you should know about this party. It'll come as a bit of a shock so you might want to sit down.'

The other boy snorts. 'Sit *down*?' He plucks at the

gold velour. 'This stuff'll split right across the arse if I do. Just tell me, and if I drop dead it's my own lookout.'

Kieran nods. 'OK, well for a kickoff it's not a posh party, and they're not paying us fifty smackers to ponce about with trays of booze. The voices you can hear through that door belong to a bunch of what the Aussies call *rock-spiders* which, in case you're not familiar with the term, means . . .'

SEVENTY-THREE

'Ah, at last!' Linton Winters beams as the twins appear in the doorway. 'Come right in, girls, it's a party. No need to be nervous.' His five guests nod and murmur, watching the pair through appreciative eyes. One who has been sitting on a sofa stands up, raises his glass in their direction and smiles. The sisters linger by the door, clearly frightened. Clare's eyes flick from man to man while Nikki, her lower lip caught between her teeth, stands half behind her.

'Oh, come *on*.' There's an edge to the host's jovial urging. 'Anybody would think we were planning to *eat* you. Have a drink for God's sake, relax.'

'Yes do.' The man who saluted with his glass picks

up a tray and advances with it. He's about forty, just starting to go grey. Clare thinks he looks like some-body's kind uncle. If she asks him, maybe he'll get Nikki and herself out of here. Instead she nods at the tray. 'That's supposed to be our job.'

The man chuckles, shakes his head. 'Not at all, my dear. Nobody here's paralysed, we're all perfectly capable of helping ourselves to drinks.' As though to prove this he plucks a glass from the tray, hands it to her. 'We're a bit on the decrepit side, I know, but we've got the use of our faculties. *All* our faculties.' His smile as he says this has the suggestion of a leer in it. Nikki shivers. The man seems not to notice. 'What we *haven't* got my dear is youth. Beauty. The beauty of youth if you like. You're here to provide that. To lend it for a while.' He twinkles. 'It's some-thing you can lend and keep at the same time, so nobody loses. D'you like the champagne?'

'I . . . haven't tried it yet.' Jesus, champagne.

'Then try it at *once*, my dear, and *do* step forward so your sister can try some too. One is never too young for champagne.'

Clare lets him cup her elbow and steer her to the centre of the room where she stands, sipping from her glass while he goes to fetch Nikki. The guests come around, smiling and murmuring, and by the time the two boys appear Clare is feeling far less ner-vous. In fact, the sight of Kieran in his flunkey suit sends her into a fit of the giggles, and she'd probably have collapsed on the carpet if the kind uncle hadn't helped her to a sofa and sat down with her, dabbing the tears of mirth from her cheeks with a tissue and giving her another glass of champagne. 'That skirt looks a bit tight round the hips for sitting,' he smooths. 'Why don't we just ease the old zip down a fraction, eh?'

SEVENTY-FOUR

As Biff Barraclough lifts the schooner to his lips, his mobile chirps. He mutters a bad word, sets down the glass and fishes the instrument out of his pocket. 'Yeah?'

'Biff, it's Charles, just checking. You did *get* four youngsters for tonight's party, I suppose? Only I forgot to mention it the other day.'

'Yeah, *course* I did,' growls Biff, who doesn't like to be interrupted at his lager. 'Your trouble, Froggy, is that you fret too much. Always did. You should know by now you can trust me.'

Flitcroft snorts. 'I trust *nobody*, Biff, that's how I got where I am. Easy on the eye, are they?'

'What you on about?'

'The *kids*, dummy. Good looking or what?'

'Yeah, I suppose. Not into kids myself but I reckon they'll do. Girls're a pair of twins as a matter of fact. Your kinky mates'll probably give you a bonus for that touch.'

There's a moment's silence. Biff sighs, wishing the guy would hang up and leave him to his pint. When Froggy speaks again he sounds nervous. 'Twins?'

'Sure, like peas in a pod. Nikki and Clare, unemployed papergirls. Go down a bomb, they will.'

'Oh, God.'

'*Now* what's up?'

'They're Pull, Biff. Your brother and his mates got them sacked.'

'So what? They don't know me, they can't connect me with you. Stop worrying.'

'I can't afford to stop worrying. My wife thinks . . . oh, never mind. I wish you hadn't mentioned twins, that's all.'

'You asked about the kids, I told you. You're getting jumpy, Froggy.' He laughs at his unintentional joke. 'Froggy, jumpy, geddit?'

'Yes, very funny. You know if I go down you're down too, don't you?'

Barraclough laughs. 'I won't expect you to do anything heroic when the bricks go down if that's what you mean. Squeal like a stuck pig, you will. Maybe it's time to get out of the kitchen, Froggy.'

'Don't talk to *me* like that, Barraclough. I knew you when –'

'Stuff it, Froggy, I've a pint waiting.' He breaks contact, drops the phone in his pocket, smiles as he reaches for the glass. *Froggy, jumpy. Nice one, Biff.*

SEVENTY-FIVE

It's cold, hanging about. Maisie tilts her wrist under a streetlamp, looks at her watch. Five to eleven. 'Shouldn't something be happening by now, John?'

Passmore's gaze remains fixed on the first-floor window of number ten. Light glows softly pink through the drawn curtain. 'Can't move till Kieran shows, Maisie.' The boy's appearance at the window is the signal they're waiting for, the six of them, hunkered in the shadow of the skip. Maisie hopes he'll be free to get to the window when the time comes. The longer they wait, the leakier the plan seems to her.

At five past eleven a car creeps into Givenham Place showing no lights. It parks in the murky area between two lamps. The watchers duck down. 'Latecomer?' hisses Lauren. Passmore shrugs.

'Hey, maybe it's the police,' suggests Penny.

Jill chuckles. 'You wish.'

'*I* wish,' retorts the big Year Twelve. 'We'd all be better off if they'd come and get us out of this job, but I don't think it's the police. Not in just one car.'

They can see pale hands on the wheel, a blob of face, but nobody gets out. After a few minutes the driver starts up, does a u-turn and drives away, still without lights. The car has just passed from sight when the curtain twitches. 'Stand by,' snaps Passmore. Six pairs of eyes watch as the pink rectangle splits down the centre to reveal a figure in silhouette. As they gaze a second figure appears and the two are seen to clash, like foes in a shadow play. Swiftly, John Passmore draws a mobile phone from his pocket, illuminates the pad and punches in the number he's memorized.

SEVENTY-SIX

It's a busy night at Sizzlers. All tables taken, a kid on every chair. Saturday night regulars keep opening the door, looking round and leaving disappointed. Gibbo peers out from his cubbyhole, frowns. *What the heck's happening? We got no promos on. No specials, two for the price of one. It's not even raining, so how come every kid in Cottoncroft's eating at Sizzlers tonight?* Gibbo's not grumbling, except he wishes his regular help was here and not taking it easy up the hospital. As long as they're buying and not wrecking the joint the kids're welcome. He's curious, that's all.

At eleven-fifteen somebody's mobile warbles and it's like a stampede. Chairs shoved back squealing, kids jumping up all over the place, running for the door. Gibbo hears the racket, hurries through to the servery. 'What's up – place on fire is it?'

'N-no fire, Mr Gibbon,' stammers the relief waiter, 'they've suddenly decided to go.'

'Have they *paid*?'

'I think so, Mr Gibbon, most of 'em anyway.'

'*Most* of 'em?' He glares at the scrum in the doorway, the toppled chairs. 'So how many free suppers *have* we served, exactly?'

The waiter doesn't know. The last clutch of kids is funnelling through the door. Beyond the big window they're shouting, sorting themselves out, surging in one direction. Bikes wobble off into the darkness. In forty seconds there's not a kid in sight. Gibbo sighs, shakes his head, begins to pick up chairs.

SEVENTY-SEVEN

'Where've you been, Charles? I didn't know you'd gone out.'

'Nowhere. Checking up on a few things, that's all.'

'That party. You're screwed up about that, aren't you? I can tell.'

'I wasn't screwed up about *anything* till you started the Holloway talk, Mavis. Everything was under control, always. Now you've got me jumping about all over the place I hope you're satisfied.'

'You know I'm *right*, Charles, that's why you're jumpy. I've been packing.'

'Packing? What're you *talking* about, you daft bitch?'

'Leaving. I'm talking about leaving while we still can, and if you won't come with me I'll go by myself.'

'Ha! *Go*, see if you can find somebody *else* who'll put you in silk and diamonds and a ruddy great motor. Talking of which, you don't take the Merc, it's *mine*.'

'You're an idiot, Charles. You think you're Al Capone because you run a couple of small-time rackets in Cottoncroft. Come *on*, for God's sake – grab a bag, empty the safe. We lose a lot but at least we're free, we can start up somewhere else.'

'I'm going *nowhere*, Mavis. I was at Givenham Place just now, checking. Everything's quiet. As far as the world's concerned it's a discreet little party in a respectable suburb, but to you and me it's worth five thousand pounds with more to come. You're crazy to think I'd run out on a deal like that.'

'You're crazy if you *don't*, Charles, but it's up to you. I'm out of here tonight and you can keep the Merc, I'll take a train.'

'Where *to*, Mavis? It's half-past eleven at night.'

'To *anywhere*, Charles, as long as it's a long way from Cottoncroft. Bye – I'll read about your trial.'

SEVENTY-EIGHT

'Hey, come away from that window, you silly . . . what're you *doing*?' Linton Winters drops his camcorder on the glass block, hurries across the room. Kieran Billings, flunkey suit awry, turns. 'What? I'm only looking out.'

'*Don't* look out. Drop that curtain *now*.'

'I don't see what –'

'*Now*, I said.' The man lunges. Kieran hands him

off like a rugby player, strides across the room and picks up the camcorder. Winters pursues, stops dead as the penny drops. 'What d'you think you're . . . who *are* you?'

The guest with Nikki hears fear in the host's tone, sits up. 'What is it, Linton, kid giving you –'

'It's *nothing*, Ken,' snaps the man shooting Ken with Nikki, 'come on – you're both doing *fine*.'

Nikki shakes her head. 'Not any more.' Swings her legs, stands, tugging down the hem of her skirt. The photographer gapes, paling. 'Yes that's right,' she sticks her face in his, 'the cavalry's here, you dirty pig. You're *dead*.' Sam Bramley, half out of his flunkey suit on the chaise-longue, grunts 'about time' and jabs a fist into the shocked face of Gordon Staples.

'OK, listen everybody.' Kieran raises the hand that holds the host's camcorder, speaks calmly.

'You're all on this, the house is surrounded and our friends have called the police.'

'You rotten little bastard!' snarls Winters. 'I'll –'

'Ah ah ah.' Kieran takes a step backward, shakes his head. '*I* wouldn't, not with the cops on the way. I'd be running if it was me.'

'He's right, Linton,' puffs the kind uncle, shrugging into his jacket. 'We've got to leave *now*. I don't know about the rest of you but I'd not survive another spell as a guest of Her Majesty.'

His fellow guests need no urging. They're already hopping about, pulling on trousers, scrabbling for shoes. Winters speaks without taking his eyes off Kieran. 'You're not *thinking*, any of you. No use running if the law has the pics I shot here tonight – they'll have us on toast. What we have to do is persuade this young man to return my property.'

'God, yes.' The uncle starts moving crabwise towards the door. 'I have the exit covered. *Get* him.'

Kieran, confronted by an advancing arc of men in various stages of undress, dodges behind the block of glass with its pills and powders. He glances about him. The door's guarded and the window is at the far end of the room. The three doors he could still reach lead to bedrooms and a bathroom, all with windows overlooking the back of the house. He doesn't know whether Passmore's got anybody round the back but it looks like his only option, and he'll need to act fast before he's backed into a corner. Beyond his adversaries he can see the twins, huddled together in the middle of the carpet like babes in the wood. He hopes they're alert enough to seize their chance when the uncle deserts his post, as Kieran thinks he will.

The men approach the block and divide like pincers, two to the left, two to the right. Winters stays dead centre to grab the boy should he try coming over the top. Kieran sees it's now or never. *It's now.*

'Watch him!' yells Winters as Kieran whirls left, sprinting towards a bedroom. He's almost caught – a hand plucks at gold velour but the fit's too snug, there's nothing to grab. Kieran crashes into the door, scrabbles for the handle, bursts through. The window's curtained, there's a bed in the way and he can feel them behind him. Desperate, he throws himself across the bed, rolls over the twins' jackets, stands. There's a flimsy-looking chair at the foot of the bed. As a fist closes on his ridiculous coat-tail he siezes the chair, drags back a curtain and rams the chair feet-first at the pane. As the glass explodes, an arm circles his waist and its owner throws himself backwards on to the bed, jerking Kieran off his feet. Toppling, the boy draws back his arm and hurls the camcorder through jagged fangs of glass into the throat of the night.

SEVENTY-NINE

They're waiting behind a rhododendron near the front door. The idea is that when Kieran tells the happy snappers the cops are on their way they'll panic, come flying down the stairs and out the door, leaving it open so Pull can go in and get their friends out. Lauren Pascoe looks at John. 'It's not working.'

Passmore shakes his head. 'It's only been a minute, maybe he's not told 'em yet.'

'And maybe he *has*,' hisses Maisie, 'and they're throttling him to death while we stand here doing nothing. I vote we smash a window, go in. And I think we *should* call the police.'

'No.' Passmore shakes his head. 'No police. Flitcroft might be the Chief Constable's golfing buddy. Evidence could go missing. This has to be an all-Pull operation.'

'Yes, but . . .' Maisie breaks off as glass tinkles somewhere. 'What's that?'

'It came from round the back,' says Penny. 'Maybe Kieran's coming out *that* way.'

'OK,' snaps Passmore. 'Penny and Jane stay here, the rest of you follow me.'

The four squeeze past the parked car and pelt round the back. It's a jungle of overgrown shrubs and grasses, pitch dark except where a lighted upstairs window throws a square of yellow on the ground. There's a door in a ramshackle porch, but it looks as though it hasn't been opened in years. Looking up they see that the window is broken. Muffled sounds reach them. Passmore cups his mouth with his hands. 'Kieran, can you hear me?' The others stand, knee deep in weeds, straining their ears. After a few seconds a strangulated voice calls out, 'Get the camera, it's down there somewhere.'

'We'll get it.' He motions to the others to start looking. 'Hang on, Kieran – we're coming in.'

As he says this a curtain is pulled aside. A face appears momentarily then withdraws. 'Quick!' croaks Kieran. 'They're coming, they'll *kill* to keep it.'

From their place by the rhododendron, Penny and Jane hear feet pounding the stairs, the scrape of a bolt. The front door is flung open and a man appears with another at his heels. 'Round the back!' snaps the first man. 'Quick.' The girls draw back as the pair dash past, making for the side of the house. They've scarcely passed from sight when there's a muffled cry and sounds of a tussle and Maisie Malin comes racing round the corner, hugging something to her chest like a fly-half going for the line. After her, in hot pursuit come the two men. It's plain to the girls that Maisie will be caught, and that what she's clutching is what her pursuers are after. At once Jane breaks cover, sprinting on a course which will intersect Maisie's just inside the gateway. As the two converge Jane holds out her arms and cries, 'Maisie, to *me*!' Maisie takes what she has in one hand, slows, and as the two men close on her, lobs it in a gentle arc toward the running Year Nine.

With snarls of rage the two men alter course, swerving round Maisie even as Jane catches the camcorder and heads for the road. As she streaks through the gateway she sees with immense relief that at least one part of their plan has worked. As far as she can see in both directions, Givenham Place is seething with kids. Kids on foot, kids on bikes. 'Grab this!' she yells to the nearest of them. 'Pass it on.'

The two men explode on to the pavement and skid to a halt. 'What . . . where the heck's *this* lot come from?' croaks one.

'Never mind that,' gasps the other, 'which of 'em's got the bleedin' *camera*?'

It doesn't take them a second to realize that the camcorder has gone for ever. They look at each other, shrug and race towards their car, scattering cheering kids.

EIGHTY

One minute there are four guys on top of him, the next he's got the bed to himself. Kieran sits up, shakes his head. Sounds through the open door. A voice raised in anger. Somebody trying to flush a lavatory without giving the cistern time to fill. Other noises, unidentifiable. He stands up, pulls a curtain aside, peers out. Dark garden, no sign of movement. Some-where a car won't start, so the plasticine's doing its job. He crabs round the bed, sticks his head out the door.

Four in the room. The host, three guests, one wearing his chinos back to front. He's yelling at Linton Winters who sweeps a handful of little boxes from the glass block and scuttles towards the bathroom. The other two, wild-eyed and dishevelled, are making for the door. Everybody seems to have forgotten Kieran. When Winters reappears, the pair have gone and Chinos starts yelling again.

'Can't you see none of that matters, you idiot, it's the *camera* that counts. I'll *happily* go down for possession of substances if they can't prove the rest.'

Winters snorts. 'It's all right for you, this isn't your place, it's *me* that'll get done, and anyway how d'you know Phil and Ken haven't got the camera back?'

'They've *gone*, Linton, I heard . . .'

Footfalls on the stairs, running. The two men freeze, watching the door, which is ajar. It flies open and John Passmore strides in, followed closely by Maisie Malin and Lauren Pascoe. They glance around the room, see Kieran, relax visibly.

'You all right?' asks Passmore.

Kieran nods. 'I'm fine but I've not seen the twins. Their clothes're in there.'

'It's OK, they're out, Sam too.' Passmore grins briefly. 'Cool kit, suits you.'

'I know. The camera . . . ?'

'We got it.' He turns to the two men. 'I'm surprised *you're* still here. Your friends didn't hang around, although I'm afraid they're on foot – didn't seem to be able to get their cars started.' He stares pointedly at Chinos. 'D'you know your trousers're back to front?'

'Five hundred for the camera,' croaks Winters.

'Get stuffed.'

'A grand, then. Two. What harm have I ever done *you*?'

'It's not you we're after, it's Flitcroft.'

'Who the hell's Flitcroft?'

'Don't shit me, he supplied the kids.'

'*Three* grand. Three grand and I'll grass up Flitcroft for dealing, look.' Pointing to the glass block where two little boxes remain.

Passmore is implacable. 'You're wasting your time, which probably doesn't matter, and ours which does.' He shakes his head. 'You're going to jail. You and all your sick little pals. The party, as the old song says, is over.'

The host looks sullen. *Don't you be so sure*, he thinks but doesn't say.

EIGHTY-ONE

It's nearly midnight and Charles Flitcroft is yawning. He hasn't slept well since Mavis's mention of Holloway and he'd probably be in bed by now if the silly cow hadn't gone off like that. She's not been a million laughs lately but the house feels strange without her and Horlicks doesn't taste quite the same when you've made it yourself. He sits in the armchair, sipping.

She'll be back. You can't get a train from Cottoncroft Station at midnight and anyway where would she go – her mother's? Not likely, the old bag's completely round the bend, wants putting down. No, she knows where she's well off, our Mavis. Big car. Designer kit. Meals out. She'll be –

The phone chirps. *There.* He grins, mimics her voice out loud. 'Charles, the last train's gone and they're closing the station, will you come and get me?' *Yes I will, but I'll make you squirm a bit first.*

'Flitcroft?' *It isn't her.*

'Yes, who's this?'

'Winters. It's all gone pear-shaped.'

'What're you *talking* about – do I *know* you?'

179

'*Winters*, you know – you sent some kids only there were others outside, a whole gang of 'em. They burst in . . .'

'Burst *in*? Were your *doors* not locked for chrissake? Couldn't you –'

'I couldn't do *anything*, Flitcroft, there were hundreds of 'em, they got a camera.'

'A . . . you mean one of *your* cameras, with . . .'

'Yes, yes, yes, we tried to get it back but they passed it from one to another. You better get your guys out, find it quick, 'cause if *I* go down I take you with me.'

'Listen, what about the police – are *they* involved?'

'Not yet. Kid said they called 'em but they never came. They fixed our bloody cars so they won't start.'

'Who, the police?'

'No, you prat, the *kids*.'

'Kids.' Flitcroft snorts. 'I can't believe you couldn't handle a bunch of –'

'I *told* you there were *hundreds*. I offered this big guy – guy of about eighteen I reckon – offered him three grand for the camera, he turned it down, said they're after you. How're *you* gonna handle it, that's what I want to know.'

'You leave that to me, Winters. I've got people all over town, they'll find your camera, no worries. Just don't panic and go blabbing all over the place, and tell your friends the same. Keep your heads down and it'll be all right.'

'It better be, that's all I can say.'

'If that's all you can say, get off the line so I can call my people.'

'OK, but remember if I go down . . . hello?' The line is dead.

EIGHTY-TWO

He's not as cool as he sounds on the phone. In fact his hands shake so badly he can't hang up and the handset thuds on the carpet. Bending to retrieve it he hits his beaker with the cable and the rug gets a Horlicks shampoo. 'Shit!'

The Al Capone of Cottoncroft doesn't call his henchmen straight away. Instead, grey-faced, he lowers himself into the armchair and sits staring at the wallpaper.

Not fair. It's just not fair. I think of everything. I plan meticulously, only to have other people let me down. They deserve to go down, I don't, and I won't. I won't. Maybe . . . maybe I should've gone with Mavis . . . NO! This is my town, my town, my town . . .

'Biff?'

'Uh . . . who the . . . ?'

'Charles.'

'Froggy? It's one in the *morning*, for God's sake.'

'*I* know what time it is, listen, this is an emergency. You know that party?'

'I *should*, you've rung me three million times about it.'

'Well, it all went wrong and it's your fault.'

'*My* fault – how d'you make *that* out, you ugly creep?'

'I *told* you those twins were Pull didn't I, so what happens? They crash the party, hundreds of 'em, nick a camera.'

'Good. You never should've got mixed up with them twisted bleeders in the first place. Serves 'em right.'

'You're not *listening*, Biff. They stole a camera, and if we don't get it back the pictures in it will send us all to jail.'

'Are you telling me they were shooting *porno pics* at this party, Froggy?'

'You *know* they were, you recruited the models.'

'I did no such thing. *Waitresses*, you told me. I recruited waitresses. If I'd known it was *that* sort of party I'd have had nothing to do with it.'

'You lying hound, you *knew*. Anyway, we've got to recover that camera before it gets into the wrong hands or we've had it, so get the lads organized, find out who's got it.'

Barraclough laughs. 'Are you *barmy* or what? You said yourself there were hundreds of 'em. It's one in the morning, they're all in bed and asleep and *one* of them has this camera. What we supposed to *do*, Froggy? Knock on every door in Cottoncroft, say, "*Sorry to bother you at two in the morning but have you got a kid who's in Pull, and did he or she bring a camera home last night, and if so can we have it 'cause it's got dirty pics of kids in it and, hey, one of 'em might just be your kid.*" Is *that* what you want us to do?'

'N-no, of course not, I meant in the morning, early. We've got records, we *know* who's in Pull. All we have to do is –'

'*You*, Froggy. All *you* have to do. See – I don't think the lads'll be all that keen to be associated with child pornographers and the guy who supplies them with talent, especially when the game's up. It's one thing to deal a bit of hash, a few pills. OK to lean on working kids for a modest contribution. That's *business*, but this paedophile stuff's something else. Totally out of our league.' He chuckles. 'And *yours*, only you hadn't the sense to see it. Night–night, Froggy. Sweet dreams.'

'Wait!' he screams into the mouthpiece. 'Are you saying Push're gonna *run out* on me after all I've done for them . . . *Biff*?'

'I'm still here and yeah, that's what I'm saying. At least, that's what I'll be *recommending* they do, Froggy.

183

After all, one of 'em's my little brother and you know what they say about blood.'

'*Blood?*'

'Yeah, that it's thicker than water. Cheers.'

'No, don't hang up. *Biff* . . .'

EIGHTY-THREE

Sunday morning. Jill opens her eyes, winces, screws them shut. Her window faces southeast and the yellow curtain hangs drenched in sunlight. The words Goldner Oktober appear inside her skull, words she read once on a wine bottle. Well it *is* October, and about as goldner as you'd want. Shame she can't just enjoy it, but it's not going to be that sort of day.

First off, she's in disgrace for coming home late last night. 'What time d'you call *this*?' goes Dad. 'Your mother's been worried sick.' The fact that Mum would've been worried a damn sight sicker if she'd known what she'd *really* been doing didn't enter into it, because Jill couldn't talk about that. She'd stood there with the camera making a bulge in her pocket while Dad tore a strip off her, calling her selfish and thoughtless, telling her she was grounded for the whole week of half-term, starting Monday.

And that's the next thing. She's grounded, so what the heck's she supposed to do with the *digicam*? She groans, curls up, pulls the duvet over her head. *I didn't ask for the flipping camera, did I? Somebody passed it to me, then I tried to find John Passmore but he'd vanished, and when that photographer came yelling and cursing I just shoved the thing in my pocket and legged it. And now I'm stuck with it.*

She can't hang on to it though, it's evidence. The twins risked their lives, Kieran got battered. She's grounded but she's going to have to get the thing to *somebody*. John said no police, which doesn't seem right, but still.

Hang on, maybe I should call *John. I mean, he's bound to be wondering who's got it, isn't he? Probably going frantic, in fact. I'll call him now, before Mum and Dad get up.*

She sits up, slides the handset across her bedside unit, pauses when it hits her she doesn't know his number. The directory's downstairs, under the hall table. Passmore. Hope there aren't too many in the book. Hope he's *in* the book, not ex-directory. She's half out of bed when the phone rings.

'H–hello?' The sudden bell has made her voice shaky.

'Is that Jill?'

'Yes, who's this?'

'Maisie, Jill. Maisie Malin. We're ringing everyone in Pull, trying to find out who's got –'

'Me, *I've* got it.'

'The *digicam*?'

'Yes, some lad gave it me. I'm *really* glad you called, I was just going to phone John.'

'I'm glad too, Jillo, you're a *star*, but listen. Don't go outside with it, we think Froggy'll have Push all over town. Hang up and John'll call you back.'

'Yes, OK and *thanks*, Maisie – I was *really* worried.'

She's just hung up when there's a knock and her father calls through the door, 'Who's that on the phone, Jill?'

'Oh – nobody, Dad. Wrong number.'

'You were talking to somebody, young woman. "*I was really worried*," you said.'

'Are you *spying* on me, Dad?'

'*What's* that you said? I'm coming in.'

He looks really angry, standing in the doorway in his bathrobe. 'A fourteen-year-old daughter comes home at midnight looking like someone who's just finished a cross-country run, won't say where she's been or what she's been doing, then gets a phonecall first thing next morning that's so hush-hush she has to lie about it.' He draws breath. 'So yes, if you like I'm spying on you, Jill, and I'll go *on* spying till I'm satisfied you're not in some sort of trouble, because I'm your *father* and that's what fathers are for.' He comes right into the room. 'I'm taking your phone away till you're ready to tell me who called, and what you were *really worried* about.'

'No *don't*.' Jill snatches at the instrument. 'He's calling me back, Dad, it's *desperately* important.'

Her father bends, jerks out the jack-plug and, gently but firmly, takes the phone out of her hands. 'If it's desperately important you must tell me about it, or your mother. Fourteen's too young to keep desperately important matters to yourself.'

She watches in dismay as he turns and leaves the room.

EIGHTY-FOUR

'Oh hello, is Jill there, please?'

'Who's calling?'

'I'm John Passmore, I'm at the Comp with Jill. She's expecting my call.'

'Is she now? May I ask what you're calling *about*, exactly?'

'Ah, well . . . it's sort of confidential, Mr Hall.'

'My daughter isn't allowed confidential calls, young man. Not at fourteen. Was she with you last night, by the way?'

'Uh . . . I'd rather not say, if that's all right.'

'But it's *not* all right, Mr Passmore. It was midnight

when Jill came home last night. *Midnight*, and she doesn't want to tell her mother and me where she'd been. Perhaps *you* can enlighten us?'

'I'm sorry, Mr Hall, I can't at the moment. I promise it'll all come out, but in the meantime –'

'In the meantime my daughter will not be available. Goodbye.'

'But, Mr Hall, you don't under –'

EIGHTY-FIVE

Ten a.m. Catherine Hall is stacking breakfast dishes in the washer. It has been a silent breakfast. Her husband is under the car where he spends most of his Sundays. Jill is up in her room, sulking.

Or so her parents believe. In fact, she's on the garage roof, which is under her window. She's in jeans and a jacket and is lying on the tiles, watching her father's feet sticking out from under the Volvo. She's wishing she was behind the wheel so she could roll forward and squash him.

When she's sure he isn't about to emerge, Jill crawls to the corner where the fallpipe is, swings her legs over the edge, rolls and goes hand-over-hand down the pipe. She's done it a few times before but she's never been this scared. Not just of Dad, though he'll go absolutely ape-shape when he finds she's defied him. No, it's Push that frightens her most. She's had an hour or two to think about the situation and she's realized there must be desperate men out there. What she's carrying in her pocket has the power to destroy their lives, so it stands to reason they'll do anything to get it back. She knows they'll kill her if they find her with the digicam, but she's got to get it to somebody and John can't contact her with instructions, so it's down to her alone. In trying to keep his daughter safe, her father has put her in terrible danger.

He doesn't know this, and so he tinkers happily as Jill tiptoes past and heads for the gate. She knows where she's going, but isn't sure she'll live to get there. In the gateway she stops, peering left and right. Four houses away, Mr Lewis is hosing down his caravan. They'll be off to the Lakes or somewhere for half-term. There's nobody else in sight. She walks past the dripping caravan. 'Morning, Mr Lewis.'

'Oh – morning, Jill. All well at home?'

'Yes, thanks.' *Wish I was off to the Lakes and you had charge of this digicam.* She turns left at the end and walks towards Thirlmere Park, keeping a lookout for lurkers. She's taking the camera to the only person she can think of who's not police, but might know how to make use of it. She's heading for the home of Dudley West, whose private address is on the card he gave her the time she went to the *Target* offices to see him.

It's about a mile. In happier circumstances she'd have asked Dad to drive her. On a weekday there's a bus, but this is Sunday so it's walk or forget it. A mile's not far anyway, but it can seem a long way if you expect to be pounced on and kicked to death every time there's a quiet stretch or a corner or a bush. Jill tries to look like she's in no hurry, not to seem scared; to act like someone out for a Sunday-morning stroll in the sunshine. There are people about but nobody she recognizes. No Push. Halfway there, still no Push. As she draws near to Thirlmere Park her heartbeat slows towards normal, the lump in her pocket starts to feel less huge, she dares to hope she'll get there.

She's under trees now, walking through drifts of fallen leaves past gracious dwellings glimpsed beyond manicured lawns. Thirlmere Park's a nice neighbourhood. It's where you live when you've cracked it; where Jill's parents will come when they win the lottery. Without knowing it she passes Mr Dick's house, its driveway hidden behind a new steel gate which clashes with its surroundings. No red tricycle will come swerving through this gateway. Not now, nor ever again.

She finds Acre Drive, walks up reading house names. *Strathmore, Beechcliff, Ty Newydd.* Gets out

West's card, checks and this is it, *Rivendell*. Please, God, let him be in.

She starts up the drive, trainers scrunching in pink gravel and there he is, raking leaves on the lawn. 'Mr West?'

He turns, frowns. 'Yes, what d'you want?' Eyes shaded by the brim of a very old trilby.

'It's Jill Hall,' says Jill, 'you gave me this.' She waves his card.

'Did I?' He leans on the rake. 'When?'

'When I came to see you. You know – about Josh Winnifrith and the Flitcrofts?'

'Oh . . . oh yes, *now* I remember.' Smiles, comes forward. 'And how can I help you, my dear?'

'You talked about libel, Mr West. Needing proof. I think there's proof in here.' She pulls the digicam out of her pocket. 'It's from a party arranged by Flitcroft.'

'Is it, by George?' His voice has gone hoarse. He pulls off a gardening glove, takes the camera, flicks the main switch to play, peers at the tiny screen. 'Good God!' He selects scroll back, gapes through half a dozen changes, switches off and looks at Jill. 'Have you . . . ?'

Jill shakes her head. 'I haven't actually looked at them 'cause I don't know how it works.'

'Just as well, my dear.' He glances down the drive. 'We'd better go inside and you can tell me how you got hold of this stuff.' He props the rake against a tree, takes her elbow, steers her towards a balustraded terrace. He seems apprehensive. She looks at him. 'Is it enough, do you think?'

'*Enough?*' He exhales sharply, shaking his head. 'It's *dynamite*, Miss Hall. These fellas – it's a miracle they let you get here alive. I'll drive you back, of course. In the meantime, you might like to sample some of Mrs West's honey cake while I think what's best to do.'

EIGHTY-SIX

The Halls discover their daughter's absence at twelve-thirty when they call her to lunch. By one o'clock William Hall has worked himself up into a quivering rage. At twenty-past the girl appears in the company of a man whose column they read every week in the *Target*. While Jill waits in her room, Dudley West tells her parents why she was late last night and what she did this morning. By the time the journalist has finished, William's rage has been redirected.

Two hours later the new target of that rage is arrested at his premises in Back Quebec Street, where he has gone to retrieve some valuable packages prior to disappearing down the motorway in his wife's Mercedes. Back Quebec Street is quiet on a Sunday, and there are no witnesses as the Al Capone of Cottoncroft shuffles weeping towards a patrol car, unless the Odeon's three wheely-bins count as witnesses.

At the police station, among other names, Charles mentions those of Biff Barraclough and Sparky Sparks, and those two gentlemen are picked up a short time later in the town centre, protesting that they've just come out of church.

The partygoers are being apprehended at about the same time in various parts of the country, having been identified through the registration numbers of the cars they abandoned in Givenham Place. All will deny having attended a party there, until next Tuesday when printouts from their host's digicam will be waved in front of them. Even then the kind uncle will swear the picture shows his twin brother.

Mr Green will never be traced. Charles keeps mentioning him, but since Green is no more his real name than Froggy is Flitcroft's, it doesn't help.

The police will not proceed against any of the younger members of Push. The feeling is that they were led astray and, since those who led them are likely to be out of circulation for some time, the youngsters should have the opportunity to mend their ways.

October half-term is not blessed with the best of weather, but there seems to be a new freshness to the air. Everybody notices it.

EIGHTY-SEVEN

A Friday night, late October. Sizzlers is busy again. Again regulars can't get a table and turn away disappointed, and again it's all down to Pull. Difference is, this time they've booked the place. Private party. This time it's official.

It's also noisy. Well, it's not every day you get to celebrate total victory over the forces of evil *and* a ten per cent rise all round. Not that anybody's actually been *given* a ten per cent rise – just doesn't happen in the world of child labour – but with no Push dosh to fork out it amounts to the same thing.

They're all here. All one hundred and forty-four of them, plus a few guests. Some came a bit late because they've been working but everybody's here now, and everybody's happy. Even Gibbo's happy, because a hundred and forty-eight customers at six-pounds fifty a head is nine hundred and sixty-two quid. *And* they've finally kicked his regular waiter out of hospital.

At ten o'clock somebody bangs on a table with a spoon and John Passmore stands up. The room quietens.

'Ladies and Gentlemen.'

'*Where – I don't see 'em.*'

John smiles. 'Comrades, then.'

'*Communist pig!*'

'Er . . . Playmates?'

'*Sssssssss!*'

'Friends.'

'*That'll do.*'

'Friends, this is a belting party, but it's something else as well. It's the final meeting of a seriously wicked organization known as Pull.'

Loud cheers, wolf-whistles, rebel yells. Gibbo cringes but doesn't poke his head out of his den – everybody's paid in advance. John shuffles his little pack of notes, waits for silence.

'Pull was created for a particular purpose, and having fulfilled that purpose has no further legitimacy. Consequently, when we leave this building a few minutes from now, Pull will cease to exist.'

'*Boooo!*'

'It will cease to exist but *we* won't, and I say this: we won because Pull pulled us *together*. We haven't been Year Nines, Year Tens, Year Elevens. We haven't been the boys, the girls, the whites, the blacks, the cools, the wimps. We've been *Pull*. We've been *one* so why shouldn't we *stay* one? Why shouldn't everybody?'

'Put a sock in it, you Year Twelve windbag!'

Nobody recognizes the voice but everybody laughs.

John nods and sits down with a rueful smile. *Year Twelve windbag.* Still in the building and already it's breaking up. He feels a pang but no surprise, because it has just dawned on him that it never was a matter of principle.

Like everything else, it was all about the dosh.